SAND

SAND

WILLIAM MAYNE

ILLUSTRATED BY

MARGERY GILL

E. P. DUTTON & CO., INC.
NEW YORK

J

First published in the U. S. A., 1965, by E. P. Dutton & Co., Inc.

FIRST EDITION

Library of Congress Catalog Card Number: 65-21277

6/66

Dedicated to
PHYSETER CATODON, ESQ.
for much kind help

I

THE shirt was made of cold cloth and frozen buttons. It lay on Ainsley's bed like a drift of snow. The cold spring wind blew the curtains and moaned under the door. Ainsley stroked the shirt. It had been starched with ice.

"Are you ready?" said Mother from downstairs.

"Are you ready, Ainsley?" said Alice from her room next door. She was ready. She was always ready.

Ainsley picked up the shirt and shook it, but that only added more cold air to it. He dropped it again and sat on it, hoping to crack the chill. It was cold again by the time he had it over his head and it touched his skin. The warm clothes he had worn all day lay on the bed. He picked up his pullover and put his face in it, to warm his skin. The cold water he had washed with five minutes ago was still damp in front of his ears.

Alice rattled his door. Ainsley put his tie on and knotted it. It pulled his collar against his neck and took the heat from that. A big shiver organized itself and spread from his throat down to his feet. It made his shoes kick his ankles, because he was still sitting on the bed, and his feet were off the ground like a puppet's.

Alice was still rattling. Ainsley unlaced one shoe and then the next, and shook them off his feet. Then he tramped his trousers down on to the floor and took the Sunday ones from the chair. They were as cold as glass too. A shiver went from his knees to the back of his neck. Then he put his jacket on, and clamped the shirt down on all the skin that had so far avoided the cold. He felt himself creeping. He had shivered his bones loose now. All he could do was shake his shoulders.

Alice was at the bottom of the stairs, pulling on a thin pair of gloves. She picked up her prayer book. Ainsley shut his bedroom door against the wind and set it moaning again. Alice looked at her watch and decided that they were not late yet. Ainsley came down and began to put his coat on.

"When will you be ready?" said Alice. "When?"

"Now," said Ainsley.

"We aren't late," said Mother. "You shouldn't be going to church out of temper with your own brother, Alice."

"It doesn't only happen when I'm going to church," said Alice. "It happens ten times a day. Now he says he's ready, and he hasn't touched his hair since last Sunday."

Ainsley looked at Alice to see whether he could find a fault with her, but she seemed to be perfect. That was her chief fault, he thought.

"It was all right this morning," said Mother, coming into the hall from the kitchen. "He's only pulled his shirt over it." She had a comb, and pulled that through his hair in its turn. Ainsley pulled his jacket sleeves down inside

8

his raincoat sleeves, and then put up his hand to stroke Mother's fur. It was her only piece of fur, and she wore it round her neck on Sundays.

"If I had fur like that," said Ainsley, "I'd be valuable."

"You wouldn't be a mink," said Mother. "Probably a rabbit." Then she put the comb down and opened the front door.

The wind came in again. It was suddenly bitter, like the sap of a dandelion. Mother put her fur against her cheek. Alice held her prayer book closer to her.

"No good sheltering behind that," said Ainsley.

"Mother," said Alice, "I wish he didn't have such insignificant thoughts."

The wind had come straight off the sea. Now all three of them were walking into it. A month ago the same wind had brought blizzards with it. Now it carried fine sand that stung the skin and then lodged in folds of cloth so that it had to be shaken out at the end of the day. If the clothes were put away with the sand in them they would moulder, because there was salt in the sand, and the salt brought damp with it. The salt and sand were both dry now, because the wind was dry. It would crack skin, and it would crack tempers too, and make bones ache. Old people and young people felt it.

At the end of the road the sea came in sight. They all three stopped for a moment, to see whether Dad was coming. He was following last of all, turning his head to the wind to lay his hair flat before roofing it with his hat. His coat was undone, and he was still wearing a knitted check waistcoat.

"Oh," said Alice. "I'm ashamed of them both. Mother, I'll walk with you."

"Now, dear," said Mother. "Alice, dear."

Alice closed her mouth firmly, and put her hand under Mother's arm. Mother put her hand across and patted Alice's hand.

9

"Ugh," said Dad, getting to the corner and feeling the wind fully on him. "It's like swallowing a knife, isn't it?"

"Button your coat, dear," said Mother. "Then we'll speak to you."

"Is it my waistcoat?" said Dad. "Funny thing, isn't it? I wonder where I got it, that's all."

Alice was made angry by that remark, because she had knitted the waistcoat five years ago, when she was eleven. Now she hated it because she thought no one wore them these days.

The sea was an endless grey, with distant white highlights scattered on it, where waves broke haphazardly. The sound of it came along the road in the quietness of late Sunday afternoon. It was like an empty sponge being squeezed. There was the noise of sand, too, rustling dry in the gutters, taking up little positions behind stones, and then skirmishing out in cross-draughts, rising up in ghostly clouds, then dropping dead on the hard pavement with a faint sigh. It would regroup in the next movement of wind, and be off again, filling the town slowly with sand.

Before they reached the sea they turned to the right. The street ran in shelter for a little way, and then there was the unsheltered openness of the level crossing and the hollow station beside it. Here the sand began. It lay thick between the rails in the station, and it filled the troughs of the crossing. When the engine came across, four times a day, to change ends of its little train, the sand would creak and groan under the iron wheels, and be thrown up under the rims and be ground to powder. There was a noise then that made Ainsley think of living teeth being filed, crumbling and cracking under a huge weight.

Beyond the station there was a little yard, swept each day so that the sand gathered at one end, not all over. The years of sweeping had raised an artificial dune at right angles to the station. The yard, though, was only half the size it had been.

Behind the artificial sand-dune there were real ones, going from the edge of the town for a mile down the coast. It was from them that the blowing sand was lifted. In the old days the station had been in the middle of the town, not at its edge. Since the railway came the dunes had moved over half the town, and buried it, roads and houses and trees. Nothing had yet stopped the sand. First it would drift into the garden, and poison that with its salt, until it was pointless to dig any more, because digging would only make the ground saltier. When the garden was given up, the sand would cover it. It would rise higher and higher, year after year, until there was a wall of it as high as the house, held back with anything that could be used. Some people had used corrugated iron, and some had used concrete; but in the end the sand would win. There would come a storm from the east that filled the gutters and the chimneys, and brought down the ceilings in the upper parts of the house, after years of filtering through the tiles of the roof. The drains would fill with sand, and water would run in from new heights, where the sand had heaped higher. Then there would be a time when it was no use carrying on, and the people would leave. A month later there would be only a dune, and no house at all.

The only building still usable in the dunes was the church. Now it stood to the east of the town, by itself. It was called the new church, because it replaced an earlier one, which had been eaten by the sand and then swallowed by the sea. The land here was first killed with the dunes, and then washed away into the North Sea. The old church had gone, five hundred years ago, and the new one would not be here much longer.

There was a sandy path down to the church. It lay low under a huge hill of sand, sheltered from the worst of the wind. It had been dug out time after time, and the sand hauled away; but the sand always came back, mounting higher and higher around it, driving out the light, withering the grass of the churchyard, and polishing the lead of the windows into a bright newness.

Even inside there was sand. It was in the books and on the tile floor; it was in the corners of the pews and it sputtered in the flames of the candles. It even seemed to be in the organ, because Mr Merriott, the organist, when he made a mistake, would pause a moment, and say loudly, "Sand in the trackers again, I don't know." Then he would skip the difficult part and go on again.

The dunes loomed up when you stood outside the church. They loomed over just as much to people who went in. They seemed even more shadowy and immense when they were seen through the obscuring stained glass. Today there was twilight coming on, and to be in church was like being in the bottom of a china cup, with a saucer over the top. There was light, but it was light with weight in it.

Ainsley wondered what prayer to make. When Alice was a lot younger she would tell him what to say. Now she quite refused, and he had to make his own. He knelt down when Alice did, and got up when she did, without managing a prayer at all.

"I didn't say anything," he said.

"That's your business," said Alice. "Prayers are a personal matter."

"What did you say?" said Ainsley.

"Just a few personal things," said Alice. She turned her head away to stop him from talking to her. At once, though, she turned it back, and began to look very carefully at her prayer book, turning over the pages at the front one at a time, without reading anything.

Ainsley turned round to see who had come in. It was Bobby Hutchinson, and his elder brother Edwin. Bobby nodded to Ainsley, and Edwin elbowed Bobby into a pew. Ainsley jogged Alice in the ribs with his elbow.

"He's looking straight at you," he said.

Alice was just about to kick him, but she changed her mind, and pretended not to know what he meant. She held her head so that Edwin could see her face, if he wanted to.

"You're poising," said Ainsley. This time he got his kick, because the word was "posing", and was true.

The sand was so near the church that the altar had been moved away from the east window, right down into the wide part of the building. During services there was nothing behind the altar at all. In the evenings it was dark there. It was like being out of doors in the woods, with the candles pale against the gloom. There was a little light shining to one side, where Mr Merriott sat at the organ, away beyond everyone else. During the service Ainsley watched the colour fade away from the big window. There was no colour left in the end, only the yellow candle flame reflected from each separate fragment of glass.

The vicar was standing in the pulpit, waiting for Mr Merriott's last note to filter away. He liked to let the music die a sort of natural death, holding the note down with his left hand and pushing in the stops gradually with the other hand. Even when he took his hand off there was still a foot on a pedal, and a note hooting. He let the note die, and then released a lever that gave an echoing thud. The vicar waited for that too, and was about to open his mouth when there was another sound.

It was a sound like gently compressed air escaping. The vicar seemed to think it was something wrong with the organ, the bellows bursting, perhaps; and he looked towards it, with an expression on his face that meant, "This is the sort of thing that happens to old organs that haven't been repaired for eighty years." Then he stood quite still, and listened harder. The noise was changing. It was no longer like a leaky bellows. It was like a cart-wheel turning in deep crisp snow, but very much louder, almost as if the wheel were six inches from the hearer's ear. Then the noise was a roar. It said what a lion would say, and continued to

13

say it. Ainsley had just time to think that it was like a load of gravel being tipped from a lorry. Then everyone realized that it was almost that. There was a heavy thud, and something hit the outside of the church and shook it very thoroughly so that the lamps swung and the candles faltered. Then there was a crumbling sound, and the bottom half of the east window was pushed in, and a brown tide of sand came on, scattering the tinkling coloured glass in front of it on the tiles. There was a wump of wind, and the candles went out. They would have been out in a moment in any case, because Mr Merriott put them out as the sermon started, on his way back to his place. Usually he would walk graciously across with the extinguisher. Today, as the noise of the break-in stopped there was a squeal from the organ, as he trod on it, and he came hurrying out and ran across the church, and sat in his place.

The vicar leaned out from the pulpit and said, "Sand in the trackers, Mr Merriott?"

Mr Merriott stood up and sat down again. The vicar said, "Let us pray," and said the Blessing, and finished the service straight away. He came down from the pulpit and switched on the chancel lights, and everybody came forward to see what had happened.

"I was frightened," said Mr Merriott. "I was plain frightened."

"If anyone else had moved, I'd have been out of the door before them," said Dad.

"Not before me, Mr Sharp," said Mr Merriott. "If I hadn't lost my way I'd be out there now. Sand. I hate it."

When they went outside it was easy to see what had happened. The top of the dune at the east end of the church had slipped down against the church wall, so that there was now a smooth slope from the peak to the middle of the east window. The wall had stopped most of the slide, but half of it had gone right through the glass, and what followed had heaped itself half as high again, and then flowed round the end of the church. The building now looked half buried.

"I hope it won't look so bad in daylight," said the vicar. "But I think it will."

"We've been waiting for it," said Dad. "It's been near for a long time."

"All that pretty glass," said Mother. "Broken to little pieces."

The vicar said nothing, because he had always refused to like the glass. A scurry of sand came whirling down the dune and licked into open eyes. The vicar thought they had better move away until the slip had settled itself. Another fall could cover them all up and leave the church like an abandoned ship, with all the lights on and the organ pumping itself, and not even a collection taken.

"Thought we'd gone," said Bobby Hutchinson, leaving his brother and coming over to Ainsley.

15

"Not quite, Bobby," said Mother. "Now, where's Alice? She's gone."

"Not far, Mrs Sharp," said Bobby. He looked back over his shoulder, to where Alice was talking to Edwin.

"Well," said Mother, "she can find her own way home, I think. And I expect Edwin can, too, Bobby, so you might as well walk along with us."

"I don't mind walking along with Alice," said Bobby.

"You come along," said Mother. "You walk along with me."

"We're left to ourselves again, Ainsley," said Dad. "Never mind. We'll sing all the way home."

II

THERE was a red polyanthus with sand in its throat. Alice took her fingers out of her pocket, into the same cold wind as yesterday, and tipped the flower's head. Ainsley tried to hurry on without her, but she caught up with him, flicking sand from her fingers. Mother always sent them off to school together, and Alice always insisted on walking part of the way with him; at least until the end of the road, whilst Mother was watching. After that she did not really want to be seen with him, and he did not want to be mothered along by her. She was very severe at times.

"Put your cap straight," she said.

"I'm not a clump-head," said Ainsley. "I don't want to look like an old sack."

"You don't," said Alice. "You look like the old potato that came out of it. Walk up a bit."

Ainsley walked beside her until the end of the road, and then they both turned right. Alice walked on. She wanted Ainsley to be disciplined, but she did not want to be with him. Some sort of remote control would have suited her, so that she could turn a switch and make him obey from the next street. Ainsley stood under a hedge, with the wind licking the back of his socks, and waited for someone to come along.

Bobby Hutchinson was the next. He came to stand by Ainsley in the imitation shelter of the hedge. He stood on his heels so that the pavement did not draw so much heat from the soles of his shoes.

"We'll wait for one more," said Bobby. "Where's Alice?"

"Gone on," said Ainsley. "Why?"

"Just wondered," said Bobby.

"I wouldn't be here if she hadn't," said Ainsley. "I'm meant to walk on with her and see her to school."

"It's funny about people with sisters," said Bobby. "You'd think they'd like them, you know. They're girls, aren't they?"

"They're not quite girls," said Ainsley. "And if you do meet any girls, then they talk to her, and what's the good of that?"

"You see, you don't like her," said Bobby. "And I think she's marvellous."

"I know," said Ainsley. "But you're a world-famous idiot, with branches in every city."

Bobby found a drift of sand with his foot, and wrote ALICE on it with his heel. The wind came and took the word away and spread it all over the town. "Even nature's against me," he said. "I wish I had a sister like her, or a friend."

"Take her," said Ainsley. "What does Edwin say?"

"We always think alike," said Bobby. "Of course."

"An old screaming hag like Alice," said Ainsley. "Here's Harold Harold Harold."

Harold Tewgon was rather precise about things. He set off from home at exactly the same time each day, down to the nearest second, and passed each point on the route to school at the same time each day. He had always done it. Even when he had first come up to the Modern school he had set out at the same time for that as he had for the Primary. The Modern school was twice as far away, though, and for his first year he had been late each day, because he could not bear to change his time-table for such a small thing. He was called Harold Harold Harold because his exercise books generally had his name written two or three times on them, in gradually better writing.

Now he came past, looked at his watch, and walked on. Ainsley and Bobby joined him.

"Fifth of a second late," said Ainsley. "By my watch." Harold walked a little quicker, then slowed again.

"You haven't ever had a watch," he said.

18

"Don't need one," said Ainsley. "Just take my time from you."

Harold's little spurt had put him ahead of time by the end of the road. He stood by the pillar-box and waited for three seconds, and then was ready to start again.

"I've got an idea," he said. "If we stop at the next corner for one and three-quarter minutes, then we shall have to take a short cut."

"No," said Ainsley. "I won't take a short cut. And Bobby doesn't want to, do you?"

"I do," said Bobby. "But I don't know a good reason."

"I know a very good reason," said Ainsley, "but I don't know a good excuse."

The short cut Harold had in mind was through the yard of the Girls' Grammar school. A detour through that cut off a long corner; but of course it was forbidden.

"But, you see, we mustn't be late," said Harold. "We only just get there in time now, don't we?"

"Exactly five to and ten and three-eighths seconds," said Bobby.

"Exactly five to," said Harold. "Not any seconds."

"I daren't go through," said Ainsley.

"I dare," said Bobby.

"I would have to," said Harold, "if I got to be that late."

Ainsley weighed the risk against the consequences. It was not easy to do, because he had no idea what the consequences would be. "We'd want a better excuse," he said. "If we did it tomorrow I could take Alice her glove, or something."

"Man," said Bobby, "that's not adventure. It's not daring. It's not brave."

"Who said brave?" said Ainsley. "I dare do it, if I wanted. But I don't want to."

Then they came to the corner. Harold stopped, and

19

looked at his watch. "One and three-quarters," he said. "Then we'll just walk slap through."

"In a busy sort of way," said Bobby.

"Have you got time to buy false beards?" said Ainsley. "I daren't go without."

"There's no point in going disguised," said Harold. "We've got to look brave. No one can get us for it, you see, because we haven't got to be late for school, and we've got to go in an orderly way, not running through the High Street knocking people down."

"Not a good reason," said Ainsley.

Bobby stepped off the pavement with one foot. Then he put his arms round the pillar-box and stood on one leg. "Oh, my ankle," he said. "Oh, my ankle. You'll have to carry me, boys. I can't walk on my own."

"What have you done to it?" said Ainsley.

"Nothing, you top-speed barbarian," said Bobby. "But it's broken, and you'll have to help me. Kind friends help wounded hero. Alice might come and bathe it for me."

"She wouldn't find much wrong with it," said Ainsley. "I think it had better have a bruise on it." He raised his foot, and kicked at Bobby's ankle. Bobby raised his foot in the air. It was the foot he was standing on, and he slid down on to the pavement and sat there. Ainsley's toe hit the pillar-box and a hollow boom came from it. At the same moment a Post Office van stopped at the corner, and a postman got out with his singing bunch of keys.

"Out of the way," he said. "You shouldn't be climbing pillar-boxes at your age, nor be kicking lumps of paint off them either."

Bobby got up, rubbing both ankles. "Seriously bad now," he said.

Harold was looking at his watch and reading the plate on the pillar-box. "Are you always seven and a half minutes late?" he said.

20

"Less of your blasted cheek," said the postman. "It's a state secret, anyway, is the Royal Mail."

"It's all right," said Ainsley. "He lives by the minute. He can't help it."

"Every hour his mouth opens and a cuckoo flies out," said Bobby. "Which leg did I break?"

The postman pulled the letters out of the throat of the box, changed the collection number on the label, and locked the door again.

"Off we go," said Harold. "We'll help our friend."

The friend managed to walk by himself, groaning as he went, until they came to the gate of the Grammar school. Then Harold looked at his watch again, and put on a tiny expression of surprise.

"No one will see that," said Bobby. "You've got to put your hand on your forehead and look distracted, and I'll put my hand on my ankle and look fractured, and Ainsley can say, 'Why not go through this yard?'"

"We've done all that," said Ainsley. "Now let's run like heck through the High Street."

"Give me your arm, Capting," said Bobby. "Colonel, you take the other."

"It's a perfect alibi," said Harold. He took Bobby's arm and held it round his own neck. Ainsley took the other one.

"Now keep your eyes skinned," said Bobby.

"What for?" said Ainsley.

"Girls, of course," said Bobby. "Especially Alice."

"Especially not Alice," said Ainsley.

The school yard was not very busy. None of the girls took any notice of them beyond a look as they hurried into school.

"We're not causing a sensation," said Ainsley.

"My idea," said Harold, "was to get into a sort of habit of coming this way, and when they get used to us, well."

They were half-way across the yard before they were clearly recognized as being trespassers.

21

"Enemy battleship approaching," said Ainsley. "All guns pointing towards us."

"She takes them for hockey," said Bobby. "She's got her hockey stick with her."

"They've all come out to watch," said Harold. "Be very broken, Bobby."

"My trouble is," said Bobby, "I feel quite cured. I wouldn't be surprised if I ran all the rest of the way."

The hockey stick was approaching. The mistress carrying it looked very knowing. Ainsley felt that to pass her scrutiny they would have to be carrying Bobby's leg in a separate bag, or she would not agree that it was hurt at all.

Bobby began to walk faster. "Limp, you fool," said Harold.

"I've forgotten which one it is," said Bobby. "I can't stop walking unless I start running."

When the invalid began to run his helpers had to run too. They threw his arms off their shoulders and left the field of battle. The enemy battleship walked gently on in the same direction, and then stood calmly in the middle of the yard.

The boys ran on in the direction they had been going. The other gate was round the corner of one of the school buildings. When they came to it they found it shut and locked. There was no way over it, because it was a solid gate in an archway.

"Help," shouted Bobby, putting his mouth to a crack. He could see the safe street outside.

"Go back," said Harold. "Run like mad."

"She can't catch us all," said Ainsley.

"I can't move," said Bobby. "My guts are crawling."

"Same here," said Ainsley. He felt that he had used up all his steam, but that the fire was still burning, and would soon be through the boiler and he would expire.

"Stop thinking," said Harold. "It won't help you."

22

"Nothing will," said Bobby, shaking the gate.

"She'll be down here in a moment," said Harold. He pulled them by their arms to make them move.

"Get going yourself," said Bobby.

"By the left," said Harold. "Spread out."

"Split up," said Bobby. "Three each."

The way back was clear. In the middle of the yard stood the hockey mistress, like some mistress of the waves. All round the yard were the girls, cheering and jeering like the breakers on a rocky shore. The three boys raced under the threat of heavy gunfire right across the yard and into the street again. The cheering faded behind them.

"No pass, no fee," said Harold.

"No nothing," said Bobby. "Now I'm all rotted up. You've killed us two or three different ways, Harold."

"Not yet," said Harold, dashing his hair back from his face and looking at his watch again. "We shall have to run all through the High Street after all."

"What on?" said Bobby. "Call a taxi, James."

They began running, but even that was not a success. They were half-way down the street when a car stopped beside them and the Headmaster looked out. "I've told you before," he said. "No running in the streets. Now walk. *Walk*, I said, you foul Hutchinson. And if you're in school on time I shall beat you. If you aren't, I shall consider it. You know what that depends on." Then he wound up his car window and drove slowly on.

"Look at the filthy ape," said Bobby. "He's still at the bottom of the street watching us. Well, I haven't been late this term. And you haven't, Harold, and you haven't, Ainsley. So let's stand here until he's vapoured off."

"Insolence," said Harold. "You know what that is."

"Oh, not pure insolence," said Bobby. "You don't just stand there sulking. You drop your books on the floor, or you say the pump isn't working. Then they can't get you for anything."

"What pump?" said Harold. "Oh, of course, Edwin's garage pump."

Bobby tipped up his satchel, and kicked the books about in an accidental manner. By the time they had picked them up the Headmaster had gone on his way.

"Now run like steam," said Bobby.

There was still trouble ahead, though. They came into school at the end of prayers, and stood at the back of the hall. They were in time to hear the Headmaster say: "The three boys who went into the Girls' Grammar school yard this morning will stay behind after prayers. I wish to see them."

He saw them all three together. The school filed out past them, the seniors first, and then the middle school, and then the juniors, eyeing them like rabbits. Then the hall was empty, and they stood alone in it, leaning on the bars in silence.

"Can you tell a lie, Harold?" said Bobby.

24

"Only to myself," said Harold.

"Nor can I," said Bobby. "Isn't it foul?"

It was foul. There was never any tenderness in the Headmaster. That was a well-known fact; the tenderness was in the pupils. Today was no exception. There were tenderness and tingling, and a cloud of shame which lasted until break. By the time break was half over Bobby had turned the disastrous defeat into a humorous story against himself.

"It's not so bad for him," said Harold. "He's only got Edwin to hear about it, and Edwin will laugh and think it's funny. I don't know what my father will say."

Ainsley was no surer about his own. Alice would be out with the story before he got home; but there might be time to change Mother's opinion of it before Dad heard it. He knew what Alice's opinion would be.

"And it's all right for Bobby anyway," said Harold. "He's leaving at the end of the term, out of the influence of this place."

"You bet I am," said Bobby. "I'll go in with Edwin. Me and Guy and Peter will be dashing around with five-pound notes. And if we get the old man's car in our place, boy, he'll never get it out."

III

"What a sordid day," said Bobby. The school doors had swung closed behind them, and there was only the evening left. The cold wind still pushed through the streets, and never gave up its breathing.

"Before it's dark," said Ainsley, "we could go and look at the church."

"Church?" said Harold. "That's strictly religious, for one thing, and a pretty poor timekeeper for another. No wonder they're having to close the railway."

It was always understood in the town that the railway ran its trains by the church clock, which was just visible from the station-master's office. At least, the clock had been visible. Now it was said to be getting more and more out of sight, because the sand-dunes were rising between the church and the station. The more it got out of sight the later the trains started. It was said that a porter had to be sent out to look at the clock and run back in when it was time for the train to go. Soon the whole church would be out of sight of the station, and then, as if one followed from the other, the station would be closed.

"The church," said Bobby, "is entitled to strike the hour when it wants. That line, you know, nought degrees Centigrade, that goes through Greenwich."

"The Greenwich meridian," said Harold. "I know about it."

"It goes straight through the church tower," said Bobby. "Right through the clockwork."

Harold did not believe this story at all. Bobby had to take him back into school and show him the wall map, with the Greenwich meridian cutting the coast just where the town lay against the sea.

26

"What's more," he said, "it's marked on the church tower with a black line."

"We're going that way," said Ainsley. "We'll show you. There's half the church in the eastern hemisphere and half in the western one."

Their way towards the church was through the High Street again, the way they had come in the morning. Before they came to it, though, they passed the solid door that had trapped them the other side of itself when they were in the Grammar school yard.

Bobby rubbed the seat of his trousers. "I'm in two hemispheres," he said. "They're marked on me with a black line."

"I don't know why they closed the door," said Ainsley, giving it a kick. "I've never seen it closed before."

The door creaked when he kicked it, and then half of it opened and flapped heavily against the side wall. A bolt was pulled up, and the other half dropped back as well.

"Good kicking," said Bobby. Ainsley was ready to retreat. He thought he would not run this time, because he was on the safe ground of the street; but he would certainly go away. He knew the kick had not opened the door. He expected to see the hockey mistress again. But there was only the smallest girl in the school, holding a large doorkey. She stepped out from behind the second door, which had swung back on her. She had two long plaits.

"Are you going to try again?" she said.

"Less of that," said Bobby.

"*I* didn't laugh at you," said the little girl. "I thought they were mean, when you had a bad leg."

"It's a lot better now," said Bobby. He thought it might be a help to have the bad leg for a day or two longer, to attract sympathy, if any of the older girls had some to spare.

"I thought you were brave," said the girl. "We all did in our form."

27

"Thank you very much," said Bobby. "But it didn't help."

"Now I've got to hang the key up and tell Miss Palmer if you're still hanging about," said the girl.

"We aren't hanging about," said Ainsley. He knew that any story of hanging about would get to Alice, and be distilled by her at the tea-table. But he didn't walk off straight away, because Harold put a hand on his arm and kept him where he was. The little girl turned away, reached up against the wall, and hung the key on a nail. Then she turned to them again and smiled very carefully at Bobby, and walked off, no doubt to report to Miss Palmer.

"I wondered where the key lived," said Harold. "Now we know something useful."

"A few hours too late," said Bobby. "Get going, Harold. You must be hours behind schedule yourself."

"No schedule on the way home," said Harold. "Show me this black line."

"Not in the street," said Bobby.

"The one on the church, you grave case of madness," said Harold.

The wind picked at them all the way, biting deeper and deeper. At the level crossing they suddenly left the small shelters of the town, and were on the edge of the larger desolation. Behind them were the houses, beside them the station, with a black engine throwing out cold steam, and ahead the wilderness of dunes and sand. A quarter of a mile ahead there was the edge of the land desert and the beginning of the sea desert. It was like the coast of some frozen Libya; though there was not quite frost in the air at this time of day.

The church was locked. Bobby looked for the key. He thought it might be hung near by, like the one for the Grammar school gate.

"There's something about the line written inside," he said. "But it's marked on the outside."

There was a black line, painted on part of the tower. It looked like a neglected length of lightning conductor. The sand had been at it and spoilt its outline, but they could still trace it.

"I've seen it," said Harold. "What now?"

"The landslide," said Ainsley. "We forgot to tell you. It happened in church last night."

They went to look at the sandslip. More sand had coasted gently down during the night, and the dune lay more than half up the window, as if it had always been there. The summit of it had settled to a new level. When the sand moved with such purpose there was nothing that could be done about it. It had come to stay, and only time would remove it.

This part of the shore was known as the South Strand. It ran southwards for more than a mile, all desert. The swallowed-up town was only a small part of it. Under the sand were supposed to be a lake, a small village, the burial mound of a Danish chief, and half the wrecks of the Spanish Armada. The tale of the Spanish ships was well known to be a fable, but it is the sort of story that sounds interesting. There was always the possibility of finding something interesting poking up from the sand. The most usual thing was a golf ball, sliced across the dunes from the links. The golfers called the South Strand "the world's biggest bunker".

The weather was dry, so the sand was lifting. It sometimes seemed as if the wind was blowing through it from below. The whole surface of a sandhill would lift up at one moment, like a cloth being flapped, and the sand would blow like a cloak on to the next hill, and then take off again, and blow on into the town.

Whilst they stood at the church they heard the railway engine cross the road at the level crossing. The sand squealed under its wheels, and the smoke and steam blew out flat from its funnel.

29

"We could go along the lineside," said Bobby, "and wave to the train." It was not quite such a silly idea as it sounded, because on this train more than half of the Grammar school went home. If you waved to them, they might wave back. It was a remote way of talking to a girl, but it was better than nothing.

They waved today, but no one saw them. The train went on its way with its eyes closed.

"Time to go," said Harold. "Nearly."

"We'll go back the long way," said Ainsley. "I'll just have to think of something to say against Alice."

They were standing between the railway and the sea. If they went the shortest way home they would either have to cross the line and come through the back of the town, or climb the railway fence into the sidings, which were between them and the station. They all felt that they had been in enough forbidden places for one day, so they turned into the wind again and went down to the road. It was only a small road, leading down to the golf links and two or three farms and houses. It was kept clear of sand year after year, because it was cheaper to clear it than to build a bridge over the railway and bring the road a different way. It was a private road. The town council had given it up many years ago.

The boys came on to it, and walked back to the station along it, and into the town.

"I shall just have to grin and bear what she says," said Ainsley. "I can't think of anything against her, and I can't think of a good enough reason for going in the yard."

"Say the truth," said Bobby. "Girls."

"Not to Alice," said Ainsley. "I don't give her the pure truth, because she tears up whatever I say. She makes it all sound like a lie."

At home, though, Alice was not concerned with him. She was eating her tea quickly. She looked at Ainsley when he came in, but she decided not to say what had come into

30

her mind. She only decided it, Ainsley thought, because she was busy thinking of something else. She finished her tea, then put her coat on again, and Wellington boots.

"Where are you going?" said Mother.

"I'm going to see Sheila," said Alice. "She knows where there are some good fossil beds; and they're not places where old people sleep, Ainsley, so you needn't say it. We had all those jokes at school long ago. But perhaps you heard this morning. Good-bye, Mother. I won't be late. I'll just take the toffee hammer."

There was a rattle of the kitchen drawer, a thump of the kitchen door, and she had gone. Mother got up and took the used plate off the table.

"Poor Edwin," she said. "He has no chance, with all these fossils and dramatic societies and record groups and hockey matches."

"No chance at hockey matches, I shouldn't think," said Ainsley. "None at all."

In the morning Harold was ahead of Ainsley, who ran to catch him up. Bobby came running a little later, and then Guy Restall. Peter and Derek were well ahead, at the far end of the empty High Street.

"Of course, we know where the key is," said Ainsley. "We could get through whatever happened."

"No thanks," said Bobby. "And don't tell Alice where the key is. You know what it is, I mean. They're a bit of a gang together."

"She's a gangster," said Ainsley.

"He's got a sister like that," said Bobby. "And he doesn't care a bit. Honestly, it's a waste of natural resources. But don't tell her, anyway."

"Girls," said Guy. "I can tell you about girls."

"You can tell us about anything," said Bobby. "You always do. I remember when you told me all about the eight wives of Henry the Sixth, and I nearly got burnt at the stake like the wives."

31

"I distinctly heard that he married Joan of Arc," said Guy. "Someone told me a lie, that's all."

Somebody was tapping Bobby's elbow. "Stop flapping," he said, because it irritated him to be flapped at. He turned to see who it was. It was the litle girl who had opened the Grammar school gate yesterday. She was grinning at him again.

"Would you like to see my fossils?" she said.

"No," said Bobby.

The little girl took no notice of what he said. She opened the cigar box she was carrying and picked out a pebble. "That's a shell," she said.

"The shell it is," said Bobby.

"And that's an amorie or something, and that's a tooth, and that's a flint, and that's out of a piece of coal."

"I don't care," said Bobby. "Go away at once, and stop walking along near me."

"But they're for our museum," said the child. "We're having an exhibition of fossils. It's a secret."

"It sounds like it," said Bobby. "I'll tell you another one. You've just walked past the Grammar school gate."

"So have you," said the girl.

"My ankle's all right today," said Bobby. "Now, you turn round and go in. Good-bye."

"I'm glad you're all right," said the girl, closing her box of fossils. "Do you know, I think you four would make a smashing group, all singing, or something."

"Get lost," said Bobby.

Harold was tapping his watch. "Not up to time," he said. "Please."

"Someone look out for the old man," said Bobby. "I'm not going to look round or I'll get waved at. Gentlemen, that was very embarrassing."

"It's your aniline nose and ultra-violet eyes," said Guy. "You ought to be playing an alto sax."

"More likely potato sacks," said Bobby.

Ainsley had been looking back, in case the Headmaster came along. He was the one who ran into the hockey mistress. It was like running into a wall. By the time he had dodged round her the others were at the end of the High Street. He was running to catch them when the Headmaster's bellow brought him to a standstill. He had to listen to an angry blast about running into other people, and running in the High Street in general, and conduct in general, and character in general. In the end they were both late for school.

Alice was very smug at tea time. She seemed to know something she thought was important.

33

"What are you hatching, dear?" said Mother. "Don't you think she's holding something back from us, Ainsley?"

"She's keeping good and quiet," said Ainsley. "Don't wake her from it, Mother."

"I can tell you," said Alice. "It's about those fossils."

"For your secret exhibition?" said Ainsley.

"Yes," said Alice. "How did you know?"

Ainsley looked knowing, and took another piece of bread and butter.

"Look at him laying the jam on," said Alice. "Doesn't it disgust you, Mother?"

"I'm glad he likes it," said Mother. "Are you having a secret exhibition of fossils, dear?"

"Not all that secret," said Alice. "Apparently. Do you know about mine too, Ainsley?"

"Of course," said Ainsley. He said it to make her angry.

"If he knows," she said, "what's the use? We might as well write an advertisement and stick it outside the school. He can't stay silent a moment. I don't like him, you know."

"You're only brother and sister, not friends," said Mother. "You're not bound to agree."

"Bound not to," said Ainsley. "She used to be all right. She used to talk to me, even."

"I resolved never to speak to him again, after I got that splinter when I was sliding. Do you remember, Mother?"

"That wasn't his fault," said Mother. "You shouldn't slide sitting down."

"Yes, but he *told* everybody," said Alice. "Everybody. And he still tells everybody everything all the time. It's strange how he can, because he doesn't know anything."

"Except about fossils," said Ainsley.

"I don't know how he knew that," said Alice. "Sheila and I found it, and we aren't going to say anything until we've got it all out."

"All?" said Mother. "What is it?"

34

"A crocodile," said Alice. "That's what we think. How did you know about it, Ainsley?"

"I expect he's got a young lady friend in the school somewhere," said Mother. "I hope the crocodile's dead, Alice."

"Fossil," said Alice. "Its bones are made of stone by now. We weren't going to say anything about it until it was ready to be seen. Now everyone will know in about an hour's time."

"Not if it worries you," said Ainsley. "I didn't think a splinter was a secret."

"It depends where it is," said Alice.

"I won't say anything about your crocodile. What's its name?"

"*Steneosaurus*," said Alice. "*Steneosaurus* Sharp. That means I discovered it. It might be a new kind not known before."

Ainsley looked at his plate before saying what he couldn't help saying. "You're a good person to name one after," he said. "It sounds about right."

IV

THE next afternoon was Wednesday, when the two top forms played football. It was better to be playing than working at a book on a desk, but the air outside was meagre and spitefully chill. Peter Knight was in goal, and grew more and more stiff with cold, so that towards the end of the game he could not bring himself to move fast enough to save. Guy and Bobby, who were on the same side (until Peter began to be a sort of traitor), chased him all the way back to school, getting there after the others, because they had had to come a long way round. If they had come the same way as everyone else they would have been seen running in the streets. They had gone through the fields and across the market-place.

"Saw your sister," said Peter. "Gardening, or something."

"Mine?" said Ainsley. "You're welcome."

"Where did you see her?" said Bobby.

"Out in the fields," said Peter. "Digging."

"I know what it is," said Ainsley. "It's her fossils. She found a crogololoconth or something."

"Crogololoconth?" said Bobby. "Coelocanth?"

"Something like that," said Ainsley. He had remembered just as he began the word "crocodile" that he had promised not to say anything about it. He thought that "crogololoconth" would not count as giving things away. But it was not very easy to tell with Alice what would count as betrayal and what would count as quick-witted saving the situation. He thought he would have done the wrong thing.

"No more fossils for me, anyway," said Bobby. "I'm getting followed about by them."

"They've got a thing about them at the Grammar

36

school," said Ainsley. "If they're still digging them out we could go that way and watch."

"We needn't actually look at the fossils," said Bobby. "I mean, we weren't going to, were we?"

"Alice showed me the crocodile," said Ainsley. "It was only a few lumps of bone. They looked like bits of fly-over before the roads are put on it." He sketched the shape of the bones he had seen. They were pieces of backbone, and they had winged flanges and spurs that could be legs.

"Crogololoconth," said Bobby. "We must get our words right, or we can't talk to them properly."

Ainsley ran through the words he had just said, and found that he had given the animal's name away in spite of being careful. But all the same, no one had believed it, because they knew there were no crocodiles about now, and it wasn't natural to think of fossil crocodiles, any more than you would think of fossil motor-cars or toothbrushes.

Alice, and anyone else who might have been there, had gone from the diggings when all six boys reached the place.

"It's arranged in strata," said Guy, who knew things, or said them as if he did. "The top strata is the air, known as the atmosphere. The next one is the ground, known as the earth. After that there's rock and stuff." Guy always thought that what he knew was strange knowledge to other people. It often was, of course; but he always knew better.

"It goes back millions of years," said Harold Harold Harold. He was very impressed with large pieces of time, and great distances, because he worked in mere seconds. He could not even measure smaller times, because his watch had a small second-hand and proceeded round its dial too fast to be read. If he had had a watch with a sweep second-hand he would have worked in fifths of a second.

Alice had been digging in the edge of an old gravel pit. She could not have done all the work herself, because there was a lot of newly turned gravel and gravelly sand, and rows of wooden pegs in the ground. The digging went

37

back under the grass at the very edge of the pit, and the turf had been cut out and put in a stack. It was the sort of thing Alice would do.

"There must be a lot of them come and do it," said Derek. "I wonder when they come."

"How do they pick them out?" said Ainsley. What Alice had shown him had been the exact colour of the gravel and sand here now.

"Who cares?" said Bobby. "We didn't come to see dead fossils, but living birds."

"The birds have flown," said Guy. He thought it was a profoundly funny joke.

"We might just find an important bone," said Ainsley. "If we looked. We'd have a good excuse for going in then. You know, a lung-bone or something."

"I'm a bit against trying it," said Bobby. "What with one thing and another, I'm bored with this place."

He led the way out of the little gravel pit, and the others followed gradually.

"Come on," said Bobby. "Let's get down in the town."

The town was really a very small place. There were the High Street and the market-place, and one or two newer streets near the sea, and that was all. Most of the people who came to the Boys' Modern school or the Girls' Grammar school lived in the country or villages surrounding. The Boys' Grammar school was down in the next small town, and so was the Girls' Modern school. It was said that since the town would be swallowed up in sand by the end of the century there was no point in building anything new in it.

They were soon in the town and soon out of it again. Only Bobby and Ainsley and Harold went right through. They lived more on the seaward side than the others, who did not want to pass their own homes on the way back there from school.

"Train's gone," said Bobby.

38

"Six minutes ago," said Harold. "According to the time-table."

They went past the station, all the same, because that led them a long way round to their homes. Then they were on the South Strand again, with the sand flinging itself at their eyes.

"More wind getting up," said Bobby. "Edwin says there'll be a storm and maybe a flood."

"There's a way of telling when there'll be a flood," said Harold. "It's to do with the moon. It has to be a new moon."

"It is a new moon," said Bobby. "I looked at it last night."

"You should have turned your money over," said Ainsley.

"It turns over quick enough by itself," said Bobby.

They were walking on the sand now, completely in the desert. The town was out of sight beyond the dunes, and there was only the sea ahead. Along this part of the coast there was no cliff. The sea came on to a shore that lay almost at the same level as itself, which was one of the reasons that so much sand was thrown up to be fresh stuff for the dunes. There was flat horizon. The air was not very clear, either, so that the cliffs that rose north and south of the town were not in sight at all.

The tide was well up today, just at this time. The on-shore wind had brought it high, and sent on it all sorts of floating things. Most of the floating stuff was seaweed, but there was a certain amount of driftwood and box tops.

"High tide," said Harold. "But not flooding yet."

"Get some of that wood out," said Bobby. "We could use it for something. We could make a bonfire."

"Go on," said Ainsley. "Try it. You can't light wood straight from the sea."

"I could," said Bobby, when he had considered it for a

39

moment. "Especially that tarry wood. Get me a piece, Ainsley, and I'll show you."

Ainsley and Harold got a piece between them, making little dashes to the edge of the water between waves, and trying not to let the water into their shoes. They came out dry-shod, with a baulk of timber, and were holding it up to show Bobby when a wave sneaked up behind them, filled their shoes, and chuckled back down the sand.

"Give me the wood," said Bobby. "I'll dry your feet."

They brought him the wood, and he laid it on the sand. It had been in the water a few weeks, and its surface was sanded soft and fibrous. Under the cover of brown fibre there was solid wood, though. Bobby brought out his knife, and began to shave off the wet jacket. The shaving took away the wetness, and what he laid bare was dry.

"You see," he said, "I cut some kindling out of it, make my fire, and there you are."

It promised to be a long job, with one penknife. An axe would have done it faster and better. Then the knife struck on the rusty core of a nail, and the edge was turned.

"I've only got to go home and put it on the wheel," said Bobby. "It'll be as good as new then."

"You're on a desert island," said Harold. "You can't just walk home. Light up the bits you've got, and we'll get some dry seaweed and some smaller bits."

Bobby made himself a pyramid of cuttings, and put a match under it. The yellow flame blackened the wood, then blackened Bobby's finger, and burnt him.

"My hands were so cold I didn't feel that," said Bobby, looking at the cooked skin at the end of his finger. He put it in his mouth. "The wood's wet, even inside," he said. "Did I get washed ashore with any paper in my pocket?"

"No," said Harold. "But I did." He felt in his pocket, and came to the conclusion that he too had been washed up without any paper in his pocket. "I did have a bit," he said, "but I left it in the fossil pit."

40

They opened their satchels and had an inquiry into exercise books. It was not wise, on the whole, to take paper from an exercise book, because now and then there was a sudden examination of all books and a counting of pages. The books had to be complete. They were made to number the pages each time a new book was issued.

There were no volunteers to the sacrifice. No one felt like risking it. The penalty for missing pages was detention, and the price of the book. One and three was a high price to pay for a fire. So there was no fire.

"We'll have one tomorrow," said Ainsley. "Look at all this driftwood. We've got our feet wet, so there's no point in wasting the wood."

They gathered a dozen floating beams, and any amount of small pieces. Harold and Ainsley walked on the edge of the water with their trouser legs rolled up, throwing the wood inland to Bobby, who stacked it amongst the dunes. No one came along the South Strand at this time of year, and the wood could lie there safely, unless the flood tide came and carried it away. If it did, it would be brought back, and laid high and dry later on.

It was Harold who caught the large fish. It was a very dead fish, and other fish had been eating it.

"It's complete," said Bobby. "What can we do with it?"

"Would its bones count as a fossil?" said Ainsley. "I could give it to Alice."

"I could," said Bobby. "How much do you want for it, Harold?"

"Nothing," said Harold. "I'm not even going to pick it up. I'm just holding it from being washed away. It's going putrid."

"It'll make ordinary bones," said Bobby. "Not fossils, unless we wait a million years. She won't like ordinary bones."

"She wouldn't, would she?" said Ainsley. "Let's give it to her."

"Not likely," said Bobby. "Not even with a ribbon round its neck."

"Yes, but if we buried it in . . ."

"In the fossil pit," said Harold. "Anonymously."

"Without saying who it was from," said Bobby."

"Wouldn't they have a treat?" said Ainsley. "Wouldn't Alice, anyway?"

They used a flat piece of wood as a stretcher, and rolled the fish on to it. It was too disgusting to touch or lift up, so they had to put the stretcher alongside and dig it into the sand. Then they pulled the wood out of the water.

"It wants a shroud," said Harold. He gathered floating seaweed, and covered the corpse. Ainsley and Bobby took an end of the wood each, and they walked along the edge of the sea.

They met no one. The day grew darker and greyer as they went, and the sea muttered ceaselessly in one ear of each of them. The sand shifted under their feet, and the cold of the wind ate at their damp fingers.

"It feels like a funeral," said Bobby. Then he said no more, because, although he had not meant to bring anything to his mind, he had reminded himself of his own parents. He had not been to their funeral, but he knew they had had one.

They passed along the front of the town. Its lights were glowing in the hazy air. No one was on the promenade, and no one on the beach. They heard the traffic moving in the streets.

The gravel pit was dark, damp, and gloomy.

"Don't muck it about," said Ainsley. "Alice says you have to dig about very carefully, or you break things."

"We don't want to mess it up," said Bobby. "What shall we do with it? Just put it down?"

"Put it on a bit they've dug, and cover it with the gravel

they've taken out," said Ainsley. "Tip him off. Isn't he foul? Do you think we ought to take him back and chuck him in the sea again?"

"We can't get him on the plank again," said Harold. "We'd have to touch him."

"Ripe, isn't he?" said Bobby. "She won't like it."

"She'll have a spade," said Ainsley. "She can cut him up with it and throw him away. It's natural history, isn't it? It might be a new kind of cod, or shark, or something. She wouldn't want to miss it."

They buried the fish, and smoothed the earth down over it. Then they walked backwards out of the pit, scratching out their footprints. They had to do it by feel, because there was not enough light to see by.

"That's crocodiled her," said Ainsley. "Crogololoconth, I mean."

"Now get home and have a good alibi," said Bobby.

Mother sniffed deeply at Ainsley when he came in.

"I can't stay in here with him," said Alice. "He's been rolling in something, I should think."

"He's not a dog," said Dad. "Or are you?"

"Not intelligent enough," said Alice. "But he wants putting outside, all the same."

"It's my clothes getting old," said Ainsley. He had grown used to the flavour of fish in the last half-hour. Indoors, though, it became stronger and stronger. Mother sent him to take everything off and have a tepid bath before allowing him any tea. When he came down again, in pyjamas, Alice was angrily ironing his shirt and vest, because Mother was getting ready to go to the Mothers' Union.

"You can't win," said Dad. "So you might as well eat your tea and say nothing."

"Men," said Alice, banging the iron down on the asbestos end of the ironing-board.

44

"How are your fossils?" said Ainsley.

"Don't talk with your mouth full," said Alice.

"I told you," said Dad.

"No good telling him," said Alice.

"Two kids, I thought," said Dad, looking up at the corner of the mantelpiece. "Two kids. Nice number, I thought. Company for each other, and all that."

"You should have chosen humans," said Alice. "Poor Dad, are we a disappointment to you?"

"No," said Dad. "I'm on your side, really, like the United Nations."

"Good," said Alice. "I'll wash, Ainsley can dry, and you can put away."

V

AINSLEY dreamed he was in a granary, with the wheat piled high round him. The wheat started to slide, and then to patter on him, stinging him in that immense but vanishing way of hurts in dreams. It heaped itself round his feet, and then began to climb him, very quickly, until it reached his mouth.

Ainsley woke up. For a moment he was in the sand that had burst into the church; it was in his eyes and his throat. Then he woke out of that part of his dream, and he was in his own bed. The bed seemed just to have come back to its own place. There was a feeling round it of rapid deceleration. But though he was awake he was still being smothered, and the idea of falling wheat grains was still with him. He found his blankets were over his mouth. He moved them, and still there was something telling him about the granary, and about the church. He listened. There was no sound in the silent night. Nothing stirred anywhere.

Then he felt the grains pelting him, landing on his face. He put up his hand and instead of touching his face they hit the hand. It was not wheat, he thought, but sand. He tried to brush it away from himself, but the sand changed to water. It was water that lay on his cheek.

He woke up properly now, and sat up. It all became clear. He could pick out sounds now; the clock ticking in the next room, for one thing, and the wind sadly forcing the door. There was another sound too. There was hail driving against the window, like fine shot from a distant gun. There was hail coming in at the window as well, and falling on the bed. The wind had risen in the night, and brought with it frozen air from the east and north. Ainsley got out of bed, treading on still-solid hail as he went, and

46

put the window right down. He was just in time too, he thought. As he lowered it there came an enormous flurry against the glass. It left half an inch of hail on the outside ledge of the window. He could see it whiter than the frame of the window, but darker than the glass. There was morning light beginning far out over the sea.

It would be daytime in China, he thought, and went to sleep again.

In the full light of morning there was hail to be seen in the corners of the streets; hail and sand. Alice drew her elbows to her side and walked on, disregarding nature's whim of leaving slippery patches on the pavement. Ainsley skidded, and spread his arms to balance himself, and waited for Bobby or Harold Harold Harold. Harold was first in sight. He said he was precisely on time, so Ainsley followed him.

They saw Bobby in the High Street. Harold glanced at his watch and stopped. "Look at that," he said. Bobby was talking to a girl.

"Come on," said Ainsley. "Let's see who it is." He was sure that Bobby would not mind having a committee to support him. Bobby didn't mind at all, but the girl went away when she saw Harold and Ainsley approaching.

"How did you do it?" said Harold.

"I don't know," said Bobby. "We just got talking. I don't even know her name. She was talking to me. Just talking. It must have been some good, going into the yard that time."

"Not a lot," said Ainsley. "She wasn't a Grammar school type, was she?"

"Wasn't she?" said Bobby. "I didn't notice. Well, it must be me they like."

"Who?" said Harold.

"Them," said Bobby. "Well, her. There's her and Alice."

47

"Alice doesn't like you," said Ainsley. "She doesn't like me or any of my friends."

Harold, who never found anything funny enough for more than a passing smile, began to grin.

"You needn't jeer at me," said Bobby. "I can't help it."

"You're telling me," said Harold. He had seen the little girl who had showed Bobby the fossils. She was walking alongside him now, waiting to see his face before speaking to him. "Look," said Harold.

Bobby looked. He had expected to see Alice, and he had looked too high in the air the first time. He had to scan a little before locating his target.

"Ha," he said. The little girl grinned, and walked on, because Bobby had stopped. She walked on, turning round every three or four paces and smiling back at him like a flower.

"You're irresistible," said Harold to Bobby. "How do you do it? Is it your brilliantine? Or the colour of your socks? Or what?"

"It's my secret," said Bobby. "What about that stinking old fish, eh?"

"Hmn," said Harold. "Walk a bit faster. It hung on a bit, didn't it? It was hardly worth touching, the amount of trouble I got for taking the smell home with me."

"I know," said Bobby. "It was fish and chips for supper. Edwin sent me down for them, and I couldn't touch them. That old fellow we caught made all the fresh fish in the shop smell like himself. I couldn't eat a thing."

"Glad I'm not going to find him again," said Harold.

The fish was not finished with yet, though. After break there was a space before the Headmaster came to take Geography. The top form used the time to raise all the chalk dust they could round the master's desk. It was always supposed that a cloud of dust might burst into flames on its own and surprise the Headmaster a great

48

deal, without doing more than burn off all his hair and moustache, and possibly ignite his buttons too.

When the Headmaster came in he did not go to the desk. Instead he stood by the door, with his hand holding it open, and said in a voice that held no promise: "I want to see Restall, Knight, Tewgon, Betters, and Sharp and Hutchinson in my study at once." Then he waited for them to leave their desks and go out of the room. He let the door fall to behind them, and they heard him giving the rest of the form something to do.

"He's giving them a bookful to get on with," said Bobby. "What's he want with us?"

"I don't know," said Ainsley. "What have you done, Guy? Anything?"

"I can't think of anything we've all done," said Derek Betters. "Perhaps he can, though."

"It won't be anything bad," said Guy. "It's probably to go and watch another football match one afternoon. Free tea, and all that. In fact, I pretty well know it is."

"How do you know?" said Harold.

"It's Hull and East Riding versus Grimsby on Saturday," said Guy. "And he was born in one and lives in the other, so that's what it'll be."

The Headmaster came out of the class-room, hunched his gown harder over his shoulders, and led the way to the study. He walked in, sat himself down behind his desk, and said, "Shut the door."

Ainsley was last in, and he closed the door gently. He could not tell how much plus or minus there was in the Headmaster's voice. Ainsley thought that whatever it was, he was himself very much there and strangely awake. He saw the white knob of the door, and the blob of paint on its brass rim. He saw the flatness of the door, and the squareness of its corners. He saw the worn patches on the varnished floor, and the bare bones of the rug the desk stood on. He saw the world outside the window bright and clear in cold sun. He saw the dust settling in galaxies on the desk. He knew that whatever he told himself about football matches was not true. His mind wanted to think of them, but something else, instinct perhaps, told him that there was trouble ahead.

The Headmaster sat still, looking at some papers on his desk, for a very long time. It was two whole minutes, by the white-faced clock on the wall. Ainsley watched the red second-hand drop down one side and climb the other, smooth and even and powerful. Nothing would ever arrest it, it seemed.

The Headmaster spoke. "I think some of you may have seen this room for the last time," he said. It was his dreadful friendly conversational deadly voice, the one he used before he plunged in the dagger of punishment. There was a little shifting of the line amongst those standing in front of him. "Yes," said the Headmaster, seeing them move, "you may indeed wriggle. Some of you were at the gravel pits last night. Who was it?"

There was another movement in the line, and that meant that they had all been there. Ainsley smelt the smell of that decayed fish again. It sprang to his throat.

"I have here four things that you left behind. They are four notes, written in writing that I recognized at once, but signed with false names. I won't read them, because you know what they say."

Ainsley felt Guy Restall shake as he stood beside him. He had written one of the notes, Ainsley guessed. He remembered that the Headmaster had only brought him and Bobby along with the others as an afterthought. This was not their concern. Ainsley switched his mind away from what was being said. The smell of fish receded from him.

"The notes are harmless," said the Headmaster. "Silly childishness. Possibly you thought they were romantic. I can't tell. And I don't care. But what I do object to, what

50

I am going to take very strong measures about, what I think is very much more serious . . ."

He can't end up with a dead fish in that sentence, Ainsley thought. It would make us laugh. But a dead fish was not the end of the sentence.

"What I look upon as the most serious thing I have yet come across in this or any other school I have taught in, is the fact that each of these notes, each silly message that you buried in the gravel pit, is signed with my name. My signature has in fact been forged four times. Not forged very well, I must say, but forged."

Ainsley listened, but this storm was not going over him in particular. He was merely a watcher. He knew that part of him was sorry to see his friends caught out; but the other part was extremely pleased to be alone in its own skin away from the trouble.

Now the Headmaster asked for an explanation, if anyone dared give it. No one wanted to speak. The Headmaster demanded again an answer to his question: who had put the signature on the letters? He looked at Restall, and asked him whether he had done it.

Guy was silent for once. Harold was asked. He wanted to speak, but found it difficult. He managed to say "Sir," and then stuck. He was trying to think of a good lie to cover the truth, because the truth was embarrassing to tell. He was not going to tell a lie about forging the signature, because he had done it; he only did not want to explain how it was forged.

The Headmaster was waiting. "Knight," he said. "What have you to say?"

"It's a drawing, sir," said Knight.

"A drawing, sir?" said the Headmaster. "It isn't. It's a forgery, sir." There was a touch of honest anger coming into his voice now.

Harold decided to risk the truth. "It is a drawing, sir," he said. "The other way up."

51

The Headmaster turned one of the pieces of paper the other way up, and looked at it. "What is it a drawing of?" he asked.

"A caterpillar, sir," said Harold. "We just found out that a sort of caterpillar was just like your signature."

"Show me," said the Headmaster, opening a drawer and pulling out a piece of paper, and giving Harold a pencil. Harold took the paper and drew on it, and handed it back. The Headmaster made him do it again, in full view.

"Thank you," said Headmaster. "You'll have to forget about doing that. I shall beat all four of you in a minute. I may as well tell you that if you had been truly forging my signature, or anyone else's, I should have beaten you and then expelled you. I shall only beat you today. That'll be twice this week, Tewgon. Your life here hangs by a very thin thread. Anything more from you, and you will be expelled." Then he went on in his fiery manner, red hot instead of white hot, for quite a long time. He came to the end of his remarks about the fate that awaits forgers and the purpose of school and responsibilities to younger people of the older ones. Then he stopped, and said: "I suppose you are responsible for a dead codfish as well?"

Harold drew in his breath, and the Headmaster looked at him. Harold thought his moment of expulsion had come on him at once. Ainsley thought it had too. It was time to rescue a friend.

"No, sir," he said. "Bobby and I did that. Hutchinson and me."

"Did you?" said the Headmaster. "Not Tewgon?"

"No, sir," said Bobby. "Sharp and I found it in the sea and buried it there."

"Not knowing, I suppose, that the Grammar school girls were digging fossils out of the gravel?"

"Yes, sir," said Ainsley. "We knew. But it was only my sister, sir. It was for her."

"All the same," said the Headmaster, "I'm going to deal

with it as a school matter. You two will go up there at dinner time and take the fish away and bury it somewhere else."

"Straight after dinner, sir," said Bobby.

"Straight after school," said the Headmaster. "I don't care about your dinner, do I? You're going to miss that, so far as I can see."

So they did miss dinner. Ainsley and Bobby were sent back to the class-room, and one by one the others came back too, sitting down firmly as soon as they could, because sitting down at once was supposed to reduce the bruises. At the end of school the Headmaster saw Ainsley and Bobby off the premises at the double. They were not going into the streets, so they were to run all the way.

"Saved old Harold, anyway," said Ainsley.

"Poor old Harold," said Bobby. "I wonder if any of the girls will be there."

None of the girls were at the gravel pit. They came up to it in a glimmer of sunshine between two clouds. The glimmer was very short, because there was a dry gale blowing, bringing high clouds overhead in a flock. In the sunshine was standing Miss Palmer, the hockey mistress. She had her hockey stick with her.

She did not speak. She watched. She hung over them like a swaying rock. They felt she was ready to fall and crush them at any moment.

Even without her presence removing the fish was a very unpleasant business, far worse than bringing it. They had to do it with their hands. The scales slid off the flesh, which was going bad and slimy. The flesh was crumbling from the bones, and the bones were separating from each other. They had to spread their hands out under it as much as they could, and hope it would not break at a point between. There was a horrible liquid oozing from it, dropping cold from their fingers and knuckles. The smell was so bad that Bobby had to put the fish down as soon as they

53

had it up, and go and breathe a different air. He thought
he was going to be sick. He came back swallowing and
looking pale.

"Not quite," he said.

The hockey mistress tapped him with the hockey stick,
and he took up his share of the burden again, and carried
it away. They took it to the beach, followed by Miss
Palmer. There they laid it down and scratched a hole for it
and covered it over. When they had finished the job Miss
Palmer had gone. Bobby went down to the sea to wash his
hands. The tide was half out, and the waves were running

in with a big sweep, a long way up and a long way back. He dug himself a little sink and washed in that.

"Now let's go home, on the way back," said Ainsley. But even that was denied them. On the cliff stood the Headmaster, watching. They had to double all the way back to school, to get there before him in his car.

VI

ALICE looked up from the bread she was cutting. She put the knife down and dusted her hand on her skirt.

"Don't do that, dear," said Mother. "Wear an apron."

"What?" said Alice, looking at her hand. "I'm thinking of him, Ainsley."

Ainsley had just come in, with a mind ready for all sorts of attacks from Alice. She was the only one looking at him in a hostile way. Mother was pleased to see him.

"Why think of me?" said Ainsley. "I don't think of you."

"You two don't try to be friendly," said Mother. "But I suppose it's natural."

"I'm natural," said Alice. "He isn't. Anyway, I'm not blaming him for anything. I know his writing. What he calls writing."

Ainsley closed the door behind him, and sat at the table. Alice sniffed. Then she put her hands on her hips and began to take in a breath. Mother turned away from the stove, to stop her, but it was too late. Alice was beginning on Ainsley. "First you can go and wash," she said, "and then you can come back and apologize, and then you can go and move the beastly thing, and then you can give up your foul ways. And you needn't talk about whether I'm friendly with you, or whether I think you're fit to be associated with, or anything of the sort, because people who do things like that oughtn't to have any consideration at all, when they come back with the smell of it all over them."

Mother had been saying mildly, "Alice. Alice. Alice." When Alice took in a breath Mother said it again, not so quietly. Alice looked at her.

"Explain," said Mother. "You don't get anywhere by arguing when no one knows what's being talked about."

"Ainsley knows," said Alice. "He can tell you."

"You should have told me when you came in," said Mother. "If he's upset you about something."

"I didn't know it was him," said Alice. "Until I smelt him. I shall be sick unless he goes and washes."

"He is ripe," said Mother. "There's the sink, Ainsley. You wash and Alice can tell me what's the matter."

"He's been upsetting my crocodile," said Alice. "He came and dug in it."

"Didn't," said Ainsley. He slid the soap down the draining-board and let it splash into the water. The warm smell of the soap began to overpower the remains of the fish smell on his hands.

"They did," said Alice. "They buried a lot of notes, and a dreadful old dead fish."

"A sort of fossil," said Ainsley.

"A sort of corpse," said Alice. "And I dug it out. It smelt terrible. Like Ainsley. Miss Palmer had to go round to the boys' school and make them take it away. She took all the notes round there as well. They were all signed with the Headmaster's name."

"They weren't," said Ainsley. "They were signed with a drawing of a caterpillar. It just happens that he writes like a caterpillar."

"Messing about with my crocodile," said Alice. "That's what's worst."

"Ainsley," said Mother.

"We were only trying to be beastly," said Ainsley. "We don't like her, you know. Bobby does, I mean, but he's a grave case of madness. Very sad."

Mother thought they had both better say no more about it, since the matter had been dealt with at school, and any more talk about it at home would only be of the quarrelsome sort. There would be bread and water and books flying about soon.

There were books flying about at school the next day,

57

Friday, because the Headmaster, looking in at the top form, had invited six boys to the football match. Guy had been right for once; but he was wrong to think that he and Peter and Harold, or Ainsley, Bobby or Derek would go. The Headmaster passed over them, and invited the next six, without a word of explanation. The books flew against the wall and the door when he had gone, in gestures of rage.

"It comes of pleasing him," said Harold. "If you don't mind sarcastic remarks."

"We'll sarcasticate him," said Bobby. "Ainsley and I didn't do anything."

"You saved my life," said Harold. "I mean, I wouldn't mind leaving a fortnight ago, but I don't want to be expelled."

A New History in Two Parts was picked up in four parts; and *A General Geography* had become a general snowstorm. Derek picked up the casualties and stacked them away with the pages mixed. "I hope his side loses twenty-four–nil," he said. "I hope both sides do. I hope it snows. I hope the grandstand collapses just under his feet."

"Can't blame him," said Harold.

"You've been beaten into submission," said Derek. "So have I, I suppose."

"We could always go if we wanted," said Ainsley. "He hasn't bought up all the tickets."

"I don't want to watch a football match," said Derek. "It's just taking someone else instead."

"And I wouldn't go," said Harold. "We know where he is if he's there, and we can be somewhere else."

School ended a little earlier on Fridays. The influence of the week-end crept into the time-table and lopped the last lesson off. They were all out by half-past three.

"A rotten day to be out," said Bobby. "If it's like this at the match tomorrow I'll be glad I didn't go."

The east wind had risen into a storm. The wind no longer let the sand settle along the street, but took it straight through, mostly at eye level, it seemed, so that the whole town walked about with a hand to its face. If you spoke you then had to spit the sand out. With the sand came fine hail, as sharp as tacks on cheek and hand. Sand and hail were not settling where the wind blew, but drifting in the quiet places, behind walls and in the wind-shadows of trees. Where the hail lodged a moment on raincoats it would melt, and then the sand would cling to the dampness. When Ainsley had walked side-on to the wind to the end of the High Street, he had a shell of sand down his left arm.

"Don't hurry," said Harold, when they were in the shelter of the market wall. "The girls aren't out yet."

Ainsley stood by a shop door and smelt the week-end magazines warm on the counter.

"They'll be out in five and a half minutes," said Harold.

They were out in five and a half minutes. Harold and Bobby went to walk amongst them, as if it were accidental, with the idea that a sudden friendship would spring up. But all the girls were muffled up in hoods and scarves, hurrying to the train or the buses. Ainsley waited until Alice came out, and then followed behind her, where he would not be seen. She was quite capable of turning on him in the High Street and telling the whole town everything he had done since the age of five. He used to like her then, he thought. It was no use making a friend of any of her friends, because they could all look at him with a sort of X-ray eye and know about all the time past.

The tide of navy-blue raincoats sank away. In the end there were two people far ahead, Bobby and Harold, still untouched by romance. Then there was Alice, walking alone, and then Ainsley, keeping to himself.

Alice turned off towards home. Ainsley waited until she

59

went into the house, then hurried past the end of the road and caught the other two up.

"Hopeless," said Harold. "It's the weather."

"Spring-time," said Bobby.

"Late winter," said Harold. "Not spring until we get the south-west wind."

"What shall we do?" said Bobby. He had nowhere to go until Edwin came back. They were the only two at home.

"Go out on the Strand," said Harold.

"It'll be just as foul there," said Bobby.

"It'll be out of the way," said Ainsley. "I don't want to be at home with her. She'll think of something."

"I thought of something too," said Harold. "I want to walk along the meridian."

"You'll fall off," said Bobby.

"I don't mean the mark on the tower," said Harold. "I mean, walk along the Strand southwards, with one foot in each hemisphere."

Bobby thought that the meridian wasn't marked, except on the map. Harold thought they could put up a ridge of sand to show it, and perhaps think of a use for it later.

The church was desolate. The wind had sifted more sand against its east wall, and made a crescent of sand that embraced it. The broken top of the dune had smoothed itself, and there was a spray of grains coming over the top now and filtering down. Sand was filling the porch on the south side. It always did that when there was a wind. The sand had to be swept out on Sunday mornings, and often on Sunday afternoons as well. The door was locked, and they could not go in to see the sand inside.

Harold looked up at the line on the tower. "I'm going to walk backwards," he said. "Just see I don't trip over anything, Ainsley. Bobby, you make some heaps of sand where I've walked, and they'll all be in a straight line."

He had not walked ten paces before Ainsley brought

60

him down into the sand with his foot. "Give up," said Harold. "You don't appreciate applied science."

"It was applied foot," said Ainsley. "I won't do it again just yet."

Bobby scraped up sand into little hillocks along Harold's track. Harold walked two hundred yards backwards, and then stopped.

"They're in line," he said. "Now all we've got to do is make some big heaps, and we can go a long way and then get them in line, and we're still on the meridian."

Harold would have gone on marking meridians all day, but in a little while they came over the edge of a dune, and the church tower was out of sight, and so were the heaps of sand. The wind bit at them when they were high up, and they had to come down again.

"It's all right on a beach," said Bobby. "All right in summer, with nice warm sand. But this sand is cold, colder than snow. It sucks away the heat."

They banged their hands on each other's shoulders, standing in a ring to do it. They thought it would be an automatic warming process. All it did was drive cold in and hurt their backbones.

"We want a fire," said Bobby. "Where's there some wood?"

There was generally wood to be found on the Strand. They had stacked some by the edge of the sea, but they thought it was too cold to walk into the wind and find it.

"Down in the sidings," said Harold. "Plenty there."

The railway sidings had been overcome by the sand. The fence had been buried, and the rails gradually lost and the buildings broken down. The railway had brought its fence nearer to the station, and left the rest to the sand. The sidings had not been railway property in any case, but belonged to a gravel company that had long ago given up.

There was shelter behind some buffers, between the tracks. There was broken wood there too, and a supply of kindling from a dead bush. The sand had killed it but not yet buried it. This time Harold had not been leaving notes among the fossils, and he had scraps of paper in his pockets. Bobby's match had something to feed on besides itself. The little flame licked up and began to crack the wood. The smoke streamed away flat on the wind.

Harold pulled out a fence post and kicked it in two. He edged the fire on to the rail, between two sleepers. He thought that the heat would spread and give them something warm to sit on.

They nursed the fire and warmed their hands. The rail stayed cold, and gradually only their hands were warm, and there were sand and smoke in their eyes.

The fire grew brighter, but that was only because the day was growing darker. They began to realize that they were not doing very well, in spite of the flames.

"I'm off," said Harold. "If I can walk."

"I thought of something," said Bobby. "A summer attraction. You know railways."

"I know railways," said Harold.

"There's all these spare rails," said Bobby. "If we could get some and lay them along your meridian."

"Thank you very much," said Harold. "They'd keep me warm at night."

"Hooray," said Bobby solemnly, to celebrate Harold's wit. "If we laid them along the meridian, we could give train rides to visitors, you know, down the centre of the earth, sort of thing. It's like an up-and-down equator, isn't it?"

"All the way?" said Ainsley.

"Just along the Strand," said Bobby. "Edwin could make a sort of engine to pull it. It could just be one rail, then we could go exactly along it."

Harold put his hands on the rail they were sitting on and tugged at it. "Get up a moment," he said. "I can't pull your weight as well."

Bobby and Ainsley got up. Harold let go of the rail and sat down. "You fools," he said. "The rail weighs about ten times as much as you. Your weight doesn't make any difference."

They had to jump on him for a revenge. "Mind my meridian," he said, getting up and defending himself. He put his foot on the fire and put it out. They stopped fighting and tried to reassemble the embers, but it was too late. The wind whipped them glowing away and they died separately on the sand.

"You nearly broke my back," said Harold. "There's a stone under the sand there." He kicked the place he meant, where there was only sand showing.

"A rail," said Bobby. "They're everywhere."

"It might be," said Harold.

The rail was just under the sand. It was a half-sized

63

rail, with the lower edge curved elegantly. Harold followed the curve a little way, until it ran down into sand. Then he looked for a rail to match. He found it, not far away, nearer than he had expected. Beyond it there was a pair of rails of regular size, belonging to British Railways, with their buffer-stop at the end of the line.

Harold dug down again between the rails, using a piece of wood, because the sand had long settled here and was hard. He came down to stone. When he had scraped about a little more he said he had uncovered a stone that held the narrow rail.

Bobby knelt to look. "It'll be a sleeper," he said. "I'll give him a shout."

There was only one way for a railway to go: out on to the Strand. The larger, standard-gauge lines met together at the station side, somewhere under sand. They did not want to go looking nearer the station, because they would probably have been turned away.

"Out into the desert," said Harold. "It's like the meridian, you don't need to uncover every inch."

They walked along, finding the rails every few feet. In one place they were showing above the sand for several yards. They curved gently across the Strand, going rather towards the sea. Then they met an obstacle, the road down to the golf links. The road, with its tarred surface, lay smoothly over them; and beyond there was a rising bank, where the sand had built up and was being held at bay by constant digging. Sand blew like flour on the tar.

When they reached the road twilight had come grey upon them.

"Leave it," said Harold. "Tea time for one thing, and we can look again tomorrow when we can see. It won't blow away during the night."

"It might blow over," said Bobby. "But we can dig it out again.

"And re-lay it along the meridian?" said Harold.

They turned on to the road and walked back to the town. As they came into the streets a red moon came out to the north-east and lit the landscape with an end-of-the-world colour, as if it were a dying sun.

VII

THE wind had brought a low, bitter cloud with it, and from the cloud there fell a stinging rain. Alice looked at it from the kitchen window, and decided she could bear it. She put on her coat and hat and said she was going out.

"On a morning like this?" said Mother. "You'll be parched to death with cold."

"It's deserts that parch you," said Alice. "Don't let Ainsley out. I'm going to the gravel pits to get some more of my crocodile."

"Nobody believes in it," said Ainsley.

"Isn't that like him, Mother?" said Alice. "Isn't that just exactly him? Didn't I tell him he couldn't keep his tongue still for a moment?"

"I didn't mean that," said Ainsley. "I told them something else. I said a crogololoconth, and they think it's that."

"Didn't you say crocodile?" said Alice. "Didn't you?" She suspected him very much, and he wished she were wrong.

"I said it afterwards," he said. "But they all corrected me and said it must be a crogololoconth."

"You see," said Alice, "he doesn't just tell one, he tells them all. Hundreds of them, I suppose."

"Go away," said Mother. "Go and dig, if you must. Ainsley, I'm ashamed of you, and that's that. He doesn't think it's important, that's all."

"He'd say anything," said Alice. "It's only ignorance that stops him talking all the time."

The door closed behind her, and all the air in the room moved round once and drifted to a standstill.

"What are you going to do, Ainsley?" said Mother. "I'm going shopping, if you want to come."

"I'm going on the Strand, as soon as Bobby comes, or Harold Harold Harold."

Mother was very doubtful about going on the Strand. There was a howling gale, she said, and the sand would be rising like foam, and there would be a high tide during the day, and an onshore wind.

"We shan't get drowned," said Ainsley. "We're not going near the sea. I expect we'll go and look at it. But I won't tell you what we're going to do, in case Alice hears."

"Something secret, like a dead fish?" said Mother. "I hope not."

"No," said Ainsley. "Just to prove I don't say everything as soon as I know it."

"Don't quarrel with her when she's not here," said Mother. "And no more dead fish of any description. It did upset her, you know."

Bobby was along before Harold. He had hoped to see Alice. He lumped about the kitchen, without wanting to leave it, until Mother said that Alice was no longer in. Then Bobby was ready to leave.

Harold was in the road. They waited for him, and walked on together. The wind was so strong that at corners of the road those at one side would be blown together, and elbows would tap together. Among the houses it was a thing that would happen suddenly. Ainsley thought it would be worse among the dunes of the Strand, but it was not. Even if it had been they might not have noticed it, because of other uncomfortable things.

The sand was like the death of a thousand cuts, where you are tied tightly in a net so that you bulge out, and the bulges are trimmed off with a sharp knife. The sand made its thousand cuts on exposed flesh, and the wind made its thousand with a cold knife, blowing through cloth at knee and ankle and elbow.

To walk on the Strand they turned their backs on the way they were going, like Harold following his meridian

67

yesterday. Today, though, no one had a foot to spare for tripping anyone else up. There were no sudden side-buffets in the gale. The wind came with a continuous and steady pressure. Since it had formed the dunes itself, to make its own way smooth, it blew over them smoothly. If there were little obstructions they were only grains of sand, and those it would pick up and hurl ahead of itself. The whole surface of the Strand was moving. When they looked into the wind over the sea it was hardly possible to tell where one ended and the other began, because the top was being lifted off each, and spray and sand drove inland together.

They tried resting in the lee of a dune, but there was more sand than air, even though there was some shelter. They tried resting, with their backs to the wind, in the open neck between two dunes, and found that the wind tried to shift them. They felt they had to hold on by pushing their weight into the sand. Everywhere there was too much noise for speech. They were in the throat of something that was shouting.

Ainsley thought he had had enough, after fifteen minutes of wandering backwards, but Bobby still went on. He tried to tell them something. Ainsley tried to say that he couldn't hear, but it was like trying to speak to the dentist when he has two fingers and a drill in your open mouth.

Bobby led them to the heap of wood. They had to cast about to find it. When they did find it the wind had been there first. It had done two things. It had added wood to what was already there, by casting some more up, and it had moved the heap inland in a ragged way. Bobby took the longest piece he could find, and handed it to Ainsley. Harold followed the example and took a long piece in his turn, and Bobby found himself another.

Bobby led them inland a little way, put his wood down, and started to dig in the sand. Digging was easy, but severe on the fingers. The farther down he went the larger the

68

sand grains became, and the wetter. He gave up digging with his fingers and found a piece of wood.

When the hole was deep enough he stood the long piece of wood in it. Ainsley got the idea, and dug his own hole. Fetching and carrying and digging, they put up a fence against the wind, and sat down behind it.

It was not windproof by any means, but it took the stress away. Ainsley found his back aching when the muscles relaxed themselves.

"Not bad," said Bobby. "But not very good. We'll just have a rest, and then make it solid. There's enough wood to make a hut, practically, and then there would be a roof over us for when it rains."

"We wouldn't need a roof," said Harold. "The rain's coming quite flat along the sand. It'll blow straight past us."

"Let's build some more," said Ainsley. "I'm getting cold."

They brought more wood, and stacked it behind the fence, on the windward side. The wind began at once to drive sand into it and bury it. Bobby shovelled more on to help it. All the top sand was light and dry, and could be thrown on with open hands. They covered the back of the fence, and then round into the shelter again.

There was more to do, though, before they could be comfortable. The wind was bound to get in to them some-how, apparently. When it could not come through it went round, and slapped them from the side. They had to walk along the edge of high water and find more wood. There was plenty to find. Ainsley thought that a groyne must have broken up somewhere along the coast, and sent long planks of barnacled wood ashore. It was heavy, finger-cutting stuff to handle, but very steady when they had put it upright in its holes.

When they had made three sides of a hut they could sit out of the wind. A little sand filtered down over them, but

69

it dropped instead of blowing. They brought in more dry sand, and made themselves couches.

"It's no warmer," said Ainsley. "What about a fire?"

There was firewood too. They avoided the wood with shellfish on it, mostly because of the smell if they burnt it, and because it did not seem fair to throw living shellfish on the fire. They were not like wood-lice and spiders, which could be rescued if they went on the fire with the logs. There is no way of freeing a barnacle from its burning house.

The fire was a good one. Ainsley thought that lying beside it was as good as having a meal. There was a certain amount of smoke, but not more than could be breathed for its taste rather than avoided for its chokiness.

When Harold said it was his dinner time, though, the fire was no longer as good as a meal.

"Why didn't you bring it?" said Bobby. "I brought mine." He patted his pocket, and lay back on his sandy couch.

"I didn't think," said Ainsley. "What about going to look at the tide first, Harold?"

"Of course," said Harold. "I nearly forgot that. We shan't be able to look very far that way, though, shall we?"

"When I come back I'll bring a pane of glass," said Ainsley. "I'm just making a glass-topped box to put things in."

They got up and stoked the fire, and stepped out of the shelter to go to the water's edge. They had no need to go far. The water's edge had come to them in the last hour. When they were down at the high-water mark collecting firewood the sea had been well out. Now it had gained a height they had never seen before, and was creeping in over the Strand in a flood. It was no more than ten feet from the shelter, and very little lower.

They went up a near-by dune to watch it. It was flooding in, coming too fast for the waves to break until they

70

hit the sand. The sand crumbled under the foam and made little cliffs, which crumbled in their turn, and then again were overwhelmed by the next pulse of the water.

"It's just lifting up," said Bobby, shouting against Ainsley's ear. He had to say it twice more before Ainsley heard the four words.

"Land sinking," said Harold, making a pantomime out of it. He turned away from the wind to say it, and looked back inland. Then he pointed, and began to run. Whilst they had been standing on the dune, watching the next dune being eroded, the rising water had come round behind and encircled them. It was eating away back and front of their own sandhill.

As he ran the sand crumbled in front of him. The water had come smoothly round and undercut the dune. He came to the bottom of it on all fours, bringing the side of the dune with him and making a bridge across the water. Ainsley and Bobby crossed him as he got up. The next

71

wave covered the fallen sand, and the next again cleared it away. The dune began to collapse, the sides sliding down by themselves, and the water eating them up.

They looked to one side, where the shelter was. The fire had gone, and was floating on the edge of the sea. The shelter was full of water. Even whilst they stood the few minutes that it took for Harold to dust sand from his sleeves, the water surged towards them, and they had to move away.

They moved away slowly at first, stopping to look back over the expanding water. Now and then they climbed a sand-dune to see farther. From the last one they climbed they saw the silver water fingering its way ahead, through some low-lying valley in the sand. They ran down the dune, and towards the town.

Close against the church they stopped and looked back again. They were out of breath.

"If we'd been eating sandwiches in there," said Harold. "If we had, it would have surrounded us and swilled us out there."

"If you'd gone," said Bobby. "If we hadn't taken a look, I would have been gone when you came back."

There was not much to be seen from where they were just now. The highest point was the church tower. They tried the door and found that it was open. They went in, and up the winding stair towards the clock room. The clock ticked louder as they came up towards it. The wind was whipping the corners of the tower, and making it hum, but it kept it off their faces for once. There was only the perpetual sand on the steps to remind them where they were. Even the glass in the windows was tinted pink, and gave cheerful landscapes on every side. Nothing upset the sound of the clock.

Mr Merriott, the organist, was winding the clock. He did it each Saturday, with a brass handle.

"Not up here," he said. "You boys."

"Have you seen the floods, Mr Merriott?" said Bobby. "Come up to the top and see them."

Mr Merriott took the key out of the clock and put it in his pocket. He followed Bobby up the tower steps, and out on to the thundering roof.

The wind up here was more than the naked eye could bear. Mr Merriott managed best, because he wore spectacles. The others had to cover their eyes with their fingers and look through cracks.

The whole Strand lay below. On the one side it was solid sand, except for the top smoke. Even that, from here, looked only like a delicate mist that would surely be underfoot. The Strand went down solid to the sea, and then ran off in islands at the leaden edge. The water was still rising. There was a long arm reaching in, the one that had seemed to surround them when they were walking back. Of the shelter there was no sign at all.

"It's half over," said Mr Merriott. "High wind, high tide." He had seen enough, and was on his way down again.

"It's my road I'm worried about," he said, as he stepped down and down. He was shrinking away from Ainsley all the time, but never getting any smaller. "If it fills my road, I don't know what it'll cost to clear again. It'll be the end of the links, too."

The road he was talking about was the private road that led across the Strand from near the station. His was one of the houses at its far end, so it was at least partly his road. It might be entirely his road, of course.

"Would you have to clear it all?" said Ainsley.

"Yes, I would," said Mr Merriott. "It's all mine down there, links and all. They won't walk to the links, you know, they wouldn't cross the Strand, and there's no other way. I wouldn't be able to get to my house, nor would my tenants. Yes, it's my road. Come down, you boys, come down. I'm going to lock the tower. I must go and see to the

73

road. I shall have to have the men out, and the sooner the better. I hate this sand. I hate it."

He sent them out of the tower, looked up the steps to see there were no more of them, and banged the door shut. Then he began to walk briskly towards his Bentley in the station yard.

"Better get our dinners," said Bobby. "I'll have mine here in the church porch. It's disused now, isn't it?"

Ainsley thought it probably was. No sand had yet been cleared away in readiness for tomorrow's services.

"Look out for floods," he said.

Alice was back from her fossils. "Oh, you're back," she said. "We were wondering about you. Is the Strand flooded?"

"It's dreadfully tremendously awful," said Ainsley. "The sea came sneaking round us, and we nearly got cut off, and when we looked where we were standing it wasn't there any more."

"Very well described," said Alice. "Do you know what he meant, Mother?"

"Of course I do," said Mother. "I understand every language. Do you know what you used to call gooseberries? Goosey-goosey-benders."

"Don't give her away, Mother," said Ainsley. "It's a bit mean. I expect she was only little then."

"Fair's fair," said Mother. "Give me that hair-brush."

"You wouldn't dare," said Alice. "You shan't."

"I'm not going to spank anyone," said Mother. "I was going to brush Ainsley's hair. What's it full of, I should like to know."

"Sandruff," said Ainsley. "A sort of mixture."

"Oh, I'm going," said Alice. "The conversation here is disgusting. I shall go and talk to my crocodile. Where I get love and affection."

74

VIII

"I've had plenty of practice," said Mother. "I can think of food any time of day or night."

"I can't think of the next meal when I'm too full," said Ainsley.

"I know you," said Alice. "You'll think of nothing else in about half an hour."

Mother was putting something suitable for tea in a bag, so that Ainsley could take it down on the Strand. He was asking her to hurry, because Bobby was still out there, somewhere, waiting for him to return. Ainsley felt the hot fire against his legs, and imagined Bobby shivering in the unwalled dunes.

After being inside the house Ainsley had forgotten what the wind was like. As soon as he stepped out of the house and into it again he thought it was going to pick him up and throw him over the hedge into the next garden. If he had not leaned into it it would have had him over, he was sure. It took away all the fire-heat at once. It was as if he had never cooked himself inside the house. To be in this wind a minute was the same as being in it a week, he thought. He curled his fingers into the palm of his hand, to see whether he could keep movability in them.

Bobby was still by the church. It was like coming across a hermit to meet him again. He had prospected about until he found the patch of sand that was least windblown, and there he had scooped himself a trench and a windscreen, and half buried himself. He had his arms out of his raincoat sleeves and his hands under his shoulders, and the sand had built itself against him on the windward side.

Ainsley walked round him, shivering and rubbing his nose. The nose felt that it was running, or felt that it didn't feel it was running when it was. Ainsley tried to explain to Bobby, but his cheeks kept shaking his jaw so that words would not form themselves properly.

"I'm quite warm here," said Bobby. "I've got a good burial. My legs are wrapped in paper, and that keeps the cold sand off. I'm all right if I don't have to move."

Ainsley had to move, though. He ran round the church to warm the ends of himself. On his way into the wind he was in treacle; on his way back there was a wing on each foot, making it swing wildly from side to side. He kicked his own ankles and lurched about.

Harold appeared by the station. Bobby shook himself out of his hole, leaving the newspapers behind, and went with Ainsley to meet him.

"We'll just have a look at the tide," said Harold. "It should be going down by now."

The water of the sea was retreating, but not very much. The wind was holding it up against the land, and making it lie flat as well, down here on the Strand.

"It's blowing up over the cliffs farther down," said Harold. "My Dad saw it on his way to work. He says you can feel it shaking the ground. He had to stop the van and look at all the wheels. He thought one of the axles was loose."

"Couldn't be," said Bobby. "Edwin services that van."

"It wasn't anything serious," said Harold. "Just England got a bit of a dance on."

When they had looked at the tide, lying like a peaceful lake among the isolated island dunes, they went down to the sidings again. Harold had been thinking about the narrow-gauge line they had uncovered.

"It just struck me," he said, "that I'd heard something about it somewhere. But I can't remember what. I thought I'd go and have another look and it might remind me."

They were a little way down the private road at this time, so they walked farther along it, to come out where

76

the lines met it, and to look the far side of the road, nearer the sea, as well. But the shifting sand had covered not only the road, but the sand either side of the road too. In the sort of landscape that is the same all over in any case, there is no way of telling that it has been changed, if the only change is one that leaves it looking exactly as it did before, except for covering up landmarks. The landmark this time was what they were looking for, the rails. They were under cover.

The road was partly covered too. Here and there along it there were the marks of Mr Merriott's tyres, but they were being either blown away or silted up.

"We didn't come as far as this before," said Bobby. They were well along the road now, and the buildings of the golf club were beginning to show ahead. There was no golf being played today. The only car to have travelled the road was Mr Merriott's.

"Right about turn," said Harold. "Somebody ought to have a map. Dash it all, down here we don't even know which hemisphere we're in."

They gave up searching soon, and went down to the edge of the sea again, and watched it out, with the help of a big fire. They found their old one lying on a new high-water mark, and used the site, though they could not use the wood until the fresh fire was going. Bobby went for the newspaper he had wrapped his legs in, and began the fire with that.

They found the shelter they had made before. The sea had dismantled it, and laid it in a row on the sand. They put it up again in a new place, and enclosed the fire, and made camp. They sat there until twilight set in, and then ate their tea by firelight, roasting jam sandwiches and grilling corned beef, and mulling lemonade in the bottle. Ainsley found it was very odd to have a hot fizzy drink.

The moon was up in the clear sky before they left the fire. They walked home across the invisible sand in a dying wind; out of the desert and under the street lights, over the new reefs of sand in the streets.

The morning of the next day was cold still. The air hung mist over the town, a mist on the edge of being frozen. A little longer and it would turn solid and cling to everything. Ainsley thought about it and asked Alice whether there was anything stickier than water. It was meant to be the sort of question that she could not find fault with, and that she would have to agree with. She would never tell him she did not know.

"Water isn't the stickiest thing," said Alice, straight away. "Paraffin is the stickiest. I mean, it stays on more things. Didn't anybody ever tell you?"

"I think these things out for myself," said Ainsley.

"No need to," said Alice. "They've been found out. Mother, is there any church today, and where is it?"

"Usual place," said Mother. "The vicar said he would ring the bells if the church seemed suitable and safe. He wouldn't if there was a wind, that's all."

The mist lifted and lifted, and there was a blue sky and sunshine beyond it. There were sharp shadows showing. Ainsley realized that he had forgotten about sharp shadows on road and pavement.

"Look at him," said Alice. "A great thing like him, and he has to jump about like a baby. What are you doing, Ainsley?"

"Not treading on the edges of shadows," said Ainsley. "Only in their honour, because there haven't been any for a long time."

"Hmn," said Alice. But she knew what he meant. He caught her hesitating by the shadow of a gate, and saw her walk in only the sunshine. She saw him looking at her. "Don't smile, I'm only walking in the warm places," she said. Dignity had caught up with her again.

The church bells called louder and louder. Today the

78

Strand was no desert, but a beach, with a blue sea fringing it and gulls back again over the water. The water itself was full of life, with the waves crunching down peevishly and clawing their way back to sea again. It was the sort of day when the bells ringing so close to the water might bring a merman out of the waves to watch at the church window.

The service was held in the back of the church. Mr Merriott was not inclined to go down to the organ, and he had to use the harmonium, pedalling with his feet. There were only three sorts of sound to be got out of the harmonium: a loud brassy one that made a tune sound like a herd of donkeys braying—a well-known seaside sound in summer; a soft sound that seemed to come from three miles away, and could hardly be heard above the mechanical gossip of the instrument; and a squeaky noise, very shrill, like a knife scratching a plate. Mr Merriott made as much variety from them as he could.

After the service they came out again into the bright day. There was no merman by the church; only the gulls sitting on the tower and watching.

"Dad," said Ainsley, "come round by the station. I want to show you something. Bobby, you come too."

"That's right," said Mother, "leave me in the middle. You three go that way, Alice and Edwin go the other way, and I'll go home and get dinner ready."

"You can come with us," said Alice.

"Or with us," said Ainsley. "Nobody wants to do without you."

"You'd rather have your dinners ready," said Mother. "Alice, make sure Edwin's coming. Ainsley, see that Bobby comes back with you."

Mother brought them both back for Sunday dinner about once a fortnight. She thought they could manage on six working days, but she was sure they could not make a meal when they had all day to do it in.

At the station Bobby and Ainsley climbed the sagging

fence into the sidings. Mr Merriott swept by in his car, down the private road towards his house and the golf links. Sand swirled up and hung in the air. He looked out with a sort of apprehensive suspicion at Bobby and Ainsley astride the top wire of the fence.

"We don't know what this is," said Ainsley. "If I can find it."

Sand had covered every place in the sidings. The rails showed like bones under a skin. The place looked as if no one had trodden there for a hundred years; or perhaps a thousand. There were wind ripples on the sand, where it had compacted on the surface and become firm.

They spoilt the perfect surface with footprints, and then with burrowings. They found the rails by hand, and then cleared the sand off them with their feet.

"I know it," said Dad. "It's not exactly a railway. It's a tramway. It's the same sort of thing. They have them in mines and gravel pits to bring trucks along. A horse would pull the trucks, or men would push them. There used to be a gravel pit out on the Strand, and they must have brought their gravel out to the station here and loaded it into railway trucks."

"Why not take the railway trucks out to the pit?" said Ainsley.

"I don't know," said Dad. "Think of some reasons. Maybe they built the tramway before there was a railway. Maybe they had to use smaller trucks because the foundations are in the sand, and railway trucks were too heavy."

"Where's the pit?" said Ainsley. "Is it full of fossils like Alice's pit?"

"It's no good asking what's out there under the Strand," said Dad. "You know there's everything, houses, churches, lakes, streets, trees, fields, hedges. There must be a gravel pit amongst it all. There'll be another town before long, too, church and station included."

"You wouldn't think it could get it all covered," said Ainsley. "But I know it does. It's getting the church now."

"Another bad storm, and the church will be lost as well," said Dad. "You see how it was a foot deeper all round today. It wasn't like that yesterday. It's lying on the roof and in the gutters like snow, but about a hundred times as heavy. It'll bring the roof in one day."

At home there was a big dinner being prepared. The smell of it met them far out in the town, because everybody seemed to be cooking the same food. They worked up an appetite and had their mouths watering by merely walking along the streets.

"Ah," said Bobby. "Parsnips, and Alice. My favourite dinner."

"Parsnips are all right," said Ainsley. "But I only smelt them by the level crossing. We might not have any."

"There's Alice," said Bobby. But he was due for a double disappointment. There were no parsnips at home, and

81

Alice was taking no notice of him. When he tried to bring himself to her attention Edwin was always there first, or if Edwin was not, then Mother was. Bobby was continually getting ready to leap up and help, and having to relax because he was too late.

"They're all against me," said Bobby.

"Even Alice," said Ainsley.

Bobby poured himself some gravy and breathed its rich steam.

After dinner Bobby even wanted to help with the washing-up.

"No need, Bobby," said Mother. "It's woman's work."

"I'm quite used to it," said Bobby. "I'd like to help. I like washing-up."

"It's really quite all right," said Mother. "We can manage very well."

Bobby picked up a tea-towel.

"Very well," said Mother. "So long as I don't do it alone."

Even then Bobby did not see the trap. Mother put the first washed things on the draining-board and then turned to Alice. "Since I've got such a good helper," she said, "I shan't need you, dear. Bobby's standing in for you."

Bobby had to be content with that: doing it instead of Alice. It was not the same as helping Alice when she was there.

"I don't think your mother's on my side," he said to Ainsley when they had finished. "She edges round what I'm doing."

"I told you," said Ainsley. "It's Alice. She's against people. I don't know why you want to gawp at her so much. Why doesn't Edwin bang sense into you?"

"He feels the same way as I do," said Bobby. "It must run in the family."

"A sort of infectious madness," said Ainsley. "Let's

82

leave them to it and get Harold and make another fire on the Strand."

Mother was glad to hear that they were going out. She wanted to know where they were going, and then shut the door behind them. Bobby knocked on it again, and was just going to say he wanted some tea to take with him when he remembered it was not his house. Ainsley asked for it for him.

They went to the Strand past Harold's house. He was pinning and gluing a model aeroplane, and did not invite them in. He was ready to come out himself, though, and only had to put his own tea in his pocket.

They went down to the station sidings again, and began to consider the railway. All that there was showing was the little part Bobby and Ainsley had uncovered in the morning.

"We'll open it up," said Harold. "I have an idea for a time-table for when we run trains on it."

"You would think of the time-table first," said Bobby. "So far we haven't even a truck."

"So far we haven't even a line," said Ainsley. "Only about two feet of it, anyway."

"And we're trespassing, as well," said Harold. "So we could get sent out of here and fined not exceeding forty shillings."

"Right, men, get weaving," said Ainsley. "We want this line clear through to the Pacific coast by nightfall."

"South Strand Railway," said Harold. "S.S.R."

"Sounds like Russia," said Bobby. "Or the Underground."

"It is underground, at present," said Harold, very pleased to have been able to say so.

"You win," said Bobby. "What shall we do first?"

"Start," said Ainsley. They started.

IX

THE storm had only been disguising. It had not hidden the rails very deep. When they knew where they were the boys had no difficulty in seeing them even though there was sand on top. There was a faint parallel ripple in the sand. If you swung your head whilst watching a particular spot on the sand, you could tell whether the surface had been laid level or had a long raised run in it. There was some difference of colour or light.

"I don't know what we can do with this little bit," said Harold Harold Harold. They had come along one rail from the station siding, as far as the road to the golf links. Here the rail ended, running under the tarmac. Beyond the road, on the sea side of it, there was a high bank, a sandy cliff, where the dune had been cut away and held off the road.

"Shunting," said Ainsley. He cleared the last few inches of sand off the rail and tapped his foot on the road to loose it from his shoe.

"Shunt back now," said Harold. They went back to the sidings along the other rail.

"If we had a bit of rolling stock," said Bobby. "We aren't kids, we can't go running up and down saying 'puff puff' and shrieking."

"Why not?" said Harold. "Engines do."

"Sometimes your jokes crease me up," said Bobby. "Other times I'm quietly sick in my own pocket without telling anyone."

"Give up," said Ainsley, kicking them both, because they were both on the ground by now, wrestling. "You're covering the lines again."

Harold got up and dusted himself. "It doesn't matter," he said. "We've only shown the tops of them. We'd have to dig them out properly. You can't run a railway like that."

Bobby thought they could borrow a spade or two from the station, because Peter Knight's father would be there, keeping his one-man post for the day.

Peter and his father were there, sitting by the tall cylinder of red-hot stove in the office, smoking and sipping tea. The air of the office was the same air that had been built into it a hundred years ago when the buildings were made. Since then it had been kept hot, and breathed and re-breathed, and never changed at all. The cigarette smoke in it had condensed on the walls and on the counter and on the time-tables, turning them all a tobacco-brown. The ceiling was the same colour, and so was Peter's father, and the tea they were drinking.

"Shut the door," said Peter. The stove shimmered in its own glow, and the coke in it settled a little. Mr Knight pressed the end of a cigarette against the red iron, and lit it. Fresh smoke floated on the thick air.

Harold coughed, and his eyes watered.

"It'll be cold out," said Mr Knight. "Upsets the throat."

"Not so bad," said Harold. "Your clock's two minutes fast."

" 'Course," said Mr Knight. "Railway time."

"It ought to be right," said Harold. "Nearly on the meridian."

"Company policy," said Mr Knight. "Sitting down?"

"No," said Bobby. "Borrowing a shovel or two."

"Plenty about," said Mr Knight. "Sanded up?"

"Just a bit," said Harold. "Set of rails down there."

"Company rails?" said Mr Knight.

"Those little narrow ones," said Harold. "They're not company ones, are they?"

"Not railway company," said Mr Knight. "Gravel company, tramway. Horse line, that. Horse there still?"

"Not a sign," said Bobby. "When did it stop running?"

85

"Never run in my time," said Mr Knight. "Company busted long before. Left trucks and everything, horse and all. Remember the horse."

"Trucks?" said Bobby. "Where?"

"Shed somewhere," said Mr Knight. "Want a cup of tea?"

A cup of tea seemed to be the right thing. Peter reached up to the top of the stove and brought the pot down. Ainsley had thought it was the kettle when he saw it first, because it had been boiling gently all the time they were in the room. But it was certainly the pot. The kettle was boiling on a gas-ring behind the counter, where it had boiled for a century. It had boiled away every layer of paint on the wood near by, and the steam had removed a deep hollow in the wood as well.

Even the gas flame burned with a brown dry colour.

The tea was very hot indeed, and the enamel mugs they had it from gave it a peculiar taste. It was the taste of the iron in it that stayed on the tongue. It tasted like the steam from a locomotive, with its mixture of grease and coal.

Peter had not said a word whilst they were in the room. He had been slumped in his chair like a drugged being. After a little while Ainsley began to share his drugged feeling, in the heat and old air of the room. A sort of cloudiness, a half-sleep, began to press on him. Conversation stopped. Ainsley understood why Mr Knight had given up making ordinary sentences. Only the essential words of the sentence were the ones worth saying. Instead of "There is a train due in at six", Mr. Knight would say "Next in six", and convey the same meaning.

Harold kicked Ainsley's chair. "Wake up," he said. "Peter, rouse up and get us some shovels. The more the easier."

"Three's enough," said Peter, when he had looked at Harold and managed to open his mouth and mind enough to understand and speak.

86

"Four," said Harold. "You come out and help."

"No business in here," said Mr Knight. "Get out, the lot." He lived almost alone in this room all his working day. Talk was something he was getting less used to.

Peter got up and came to the door. He took his coat off the back of the door, a scarf, and a helmet, and put them on. Mr Knight dropped his cigarette-end on the floor, trod with one foot somewhere near where it had fallen, and reached for a ledger. He opened it, dipped a pen in the inkpot, which was full only of dry blue silt, and went to sleep.

They closed the door on him and went out into the standing cold. Bobby said that his first breath out was a dull black cindery colour.

"Foul out here, isn't it?" said Peter, breathing very small breaths of the cold air.

"Wonderful," said Harold, taking a deep breath. But his lungs too were warmly relaxed, and the cold breath was sent back, with a cough to push it out as soon as possible.

There were shovels standing in different places. Some were in the yard, and were used for moving sand that had drifted in. Others were leaning in doorways, and in plate-layers' huts. There were two huts. One of them was full of firewood, and the other had no roof.

"There's all sorts of shovels," said Peter. "Some railway ones, some gravel company ones. They left all their stuff. It doesn't belong to anyone at all now. I know it doesn't, because the railway company wants to be rid of it, and they can't find the owner."

"We'll just have a shovel each," said Harold. "What about the trucks, Peter?"

"In a shed over here," said Peter. "They're no use, though, and you can't get them out. I mean, you can if you want, but you can't because the roof's fallen in."

There was a long shed with a narrow-gauge line running into it. There was a door to it, and the rails went in under the door. Round the door was a wall, and there was a wall along the side of the shed. The roof had collapsed inside, though.

Peter had the key to the door. He put it in the lock and turned it, and opened the door. Beyond it there was daylight, and Bobby walking on the roof, making sand slide down over the remains of rafters and joists.

There were trucks there, and the roof was mingled with them, and so was the universal sand.

"Don't let little difficulties thwart you," said Harold. "Get hold of that beam, Bobby, and let's have it out and over the side."

They started on Sunday afternoon. It was Tuesday night before they had the first truck uncovered, free of the encumbering wood and clinging sand. Even then it would not move. The axles were solid, and the coupling to the next truck in could not be broken free.

"We'll oil it," said Bobby. "Edwin's got some oil that cleans anything up. I'll bring some tomorrow."

"Get some oil to take all these beams off the rest of the trucks," said Ainsley. "We might be able to move all the trucks at once."

"It's just knowing how to uncouple them," said Bobby. "That's most of the trouble."

Peter was still working with them. He had set out to help half-heartedly. When he was small he had not been able to move anything in the shed, and he still did not believe it was possible. He kept saying that the worst was to come, and that they would never finish it. "I know the weight of some of those beams," he said.

Guy heard about the digging, and came to give advice. "It isn't very difficult," he said. "If you do it systemaciously. You get hold of that end, Bobby, and you get hold of that one, no, that one, you fool, and then lift, and it'll come out."

88

Harold stopped digging to watch. Ainsley watched with him. Bobby and Peter lifted and struggled. Nothing moved but the sand.

"From here," said Harold, "it looks as if they've got hold of different pieces of wood, Guy. They're sort of lifting against each other."

"I quite believe it," said Guy. "It's not worth trying to help some people. Harold, it would be easier if you put all that sand off the floor into one of the trucks, and then you'll be able to pull it out when you get the truck free. Like this." He scooped up sand and piled it into the first truck, shovel by shovel.

"Good idea," said Harold. "You might as well put it in there. I've just taken it all out, to give us a chance."

"No method," said Guy.

He was right, in a way, to say that there was no method. There was certainly no quick way of doing anything. The only way to get the trucks out was to remove the wood of the broken roof, stack it up tidily out of the way of the station's still-used lines, and shift the sand that had filled and buried the trucks. No method but persistence would do it. Guy tired of persistence. He spent half his time shaking the first truck to make it move away from the others, but rust and decay did not let him move it. It seemed to have grown solidly to the rails it was on.

From the hut the narrow gauge rails ran among the others, crossing them and wandering back to the place where they had been uncovered. Harold traced out the track, and set Guy to clean the crossings. He could use his methods on them.

It was light enough to work until nearly seven o'clock at this time of year, which gave them three hours in the day, from four o'clock onwards, if they missed tea. Ainsley had to be back no later than quarter past seven, though, to get his tea. Mother was very obliging about meals and food. She offered to have a sandwich tea ready for him to take down to his work if he wanted; but since he had only said he was moving wood at the station, and not told her exactly what they were doing, because they did not know how well they would succeed, he refused anything special. Mother said that she and Alice would have a cup of tea and a bun when Alice got in from school, and a proper tea at seven, when Dad was home. He could change and be tidy before tea for a while, instead of after. She did not mind if Ainsley was late, so long as he overlapped the meal a little. If anyone missed a meal without good reason she felt offended and hurt, as if her cooking had been rejected.

Ainsley missed tea by a long way on Thursday. They had kept time by the church clock. It had grown dark, of course, but they were used to that, and went on working by moonlight, because the moon was still large in the sky, and was still up early. The clock never seemed to strike. In the end Peter went to look at the station clock. It was ten to eight.

"I'm sure the church clock's stopped," said Ainsley. "If we wait until eight we shall know."

At eight there was silence from the church. They walked across the sand in the moonlight and looked up. The black pointers on the white face were still at ten to five. The clock had not lasted the week.

At home Mother was a little silent with Ainsley, and Alice looked at him as if he had been tearing the curtains in a temper, or done something as stupidly violent and childish.

"I can't help it if the clock stops," said Ainsley. "I didn't stop it and I can't start it."

The next morning Dad stopped Mr Merriott as he went through the town. Mr Merriott stopped with caution, ready to drive off straight away. Ever since he had bought a brand-new Bentley he had been a little nervous, in case a revolution started and he was to be the first victim among the rich. Mr Sharp looked rather different in his working clothes on a week-day. Mr Merriott was used to seeing him only on Sundays.

Dad brought the conversation home that evening. "He blames you boys," he said. "You put him off when he was winding the clock on Saturday, telling him about the tide. He didn't finish winding. He'll have done it now, though, and put the clock right."

"No more excuses," said Alice.

That evening they had all the trucks standing clear of wood and sand, but they were still immovable. Guy said that it was sheer weight that made them stand so firm; but Bobby and Harold thought there was something else to it as well. They brought oil and put it everywhere that looked at all rusty or seized up, and did a good deal of clouting with a hammer, beating flakes off the wheels and the couplings.

The next day was Friday, and there would be more time to work, and a complete week-end after the evening. At school they commandeered Derek, and went sixfold arm in arm along the High Street as the girls came out of the Grammar school. They were doing quite well, they thought, and attracting attention from the girls, when Miss Palmer came and pulled them link from link apart in two places, and made them walk more tidily. She did not say a word.

"She keeps beating us in public," said Bobby. "What can we do about it?"

"Get her on those trucks," said Peter, who had felt one of her hands on his arm. "She'll shift them. Grind them to powder, I should think."

They went round by the station, passing the garage where Edwin worked. Bobby went in and borrowed something from him. It was a lifting jack, of the kind that has four little wheels and a long handle to pump. It pulls along with a great deal of noise. They sat Peter on it, on his satchel, and pulled him along the pavement, stopping now and then to raise him a little higher until he fell off, and they started again.

"We could derail the engine with this," said Bobby. "Then no train would go. But I don't think it would help us."

"Jacking up a railway engine counts as stealing it," said Guy. "I definitely know that." Guy always seemed to know a lot of things definitely. This time he was thinking of hi-jacking.

The hydraulic jack lifted the first truck straight off the rails before they knew what it was doing. Bobby was working the handle, because he was in charge of it. He pulled the lever and let the truck down again. It slipped sideways and landed on the sand.

"Done it now," said Guy. "You have to be more gentle, you know. It's no good being violent."

He was wrong again. Derailment was the very thing the trucks needed. With six people to help they could be lifted out of the sand and put back on the rail outside the shed, where the line was in a better state. One by one they were prised from the rails and taken out. The couplings came undone as the trucks were raised, where the oil had done its work and softened the rust and deposits of old grease.

The wheels would not turn very well yet, because the oil had not seeped through to the centres of the bearing. When they pushed the first truck there was a howling like hyenas, that echoed from the station walls, and brought Mr Knight out from his office to see what was happening.

"Oil, oil, oil," said Bobby, and he poured it on. Peter went for some paraffin, borrowing it from the railway's supply. The paraffin carried the oil where it was wanted, and the stiffness and agony went out of the axles in turn. The trucks could be moved by one person, when the treatment was over. They were nothing like full size, of course. It was more like pushing a heavy pram.

93

They mastered the couplings. Until they found how to lock them the trucks would separate as soon as they were moved. They assembled them on the line outside the shed, closed the shed door tidily, because it seemed the right thing to do, and began to move the trucks on their own rails.

Guy had found where they should run, and cleared the tracks of sand and wood. The wood had been put in here and there to fill in the gaps where the narrow gauge crossed the standard-gauge of British Railways. The trucks moved easily from the shed down to the sidings.

X

"AND then what happened?" said Alice. "Or haven't you thought of it yet?"

"Alice, dear," said Mother. "Ainsley doesn't make things up. You oughtn't to say things like that."

"You know what I mean, Mother," said Alice. "He doesn't make things up, but he puts them the other way round so that it sounds different."

"What did happen, Ainsley?" said Mother.

"It's all uphill," said Ainsley. "The rails go up this hill, only you can't tell by looking, only when you're pushing. So we pushed and pushed, and we got the trucks up right as far as the road. We can't go any farther now, because of the road. There's only this little piece of track, and we think it's the shortest railway in the world. Nothing happened really. I mean, we didn't do anything. We got the trucks up there, and then we all must have let go, and they ran away. They squeak a bit, you know, and it sounded like a lot of little pigs running away, so we just listened and thought it was funny. We thought they would stop. But they didn't, they squeaked right across the lines, and went back into the shed where we'd got them from."

"It should have been all right," said Mother. "Wouldn't you have put them there for the night?"

"Of course," said Ainsley. " We were going to. But we would have opened the door first. You see, we'd closed it."

"*You* didn't," said Alice. "You've never been known to close a door in your life. You don't even close the bathroom door."

"She's getting nastier," said Ainsley. "I won't tell you any more whilst she's still here."

"I've got better things to do," said Alice. "Rather important, in fact."

95

"What is it, dear?" said Mother.

"I can't tell you when he's here," said Alice. "Because he's sure to tell everybody. And that's true, isn't it? But I might be . . . Well, I won't say; but you'll be pleased, I expect."

"You're both better one at a time," said Mother. "And I want to hear about the railway, even if you don't."

"I do," said Alice. "But I'm not going to apologize."

She went out. She carefully closed the door behind her.

"Now I'll go on," said Ainsley. "You see, they didn't break the door, because it was a good catch. They went rushing through the whole wall, because it was only a wooden one; and then they climbed up on themselves and just sort of died in a heap. They were all tangled up. Mr Knight came running out, to see what it was."

"What did he say?" said Mother. "Was he angry?"

"No," said Ainsley. "They aren't anyone's trucks. They don't belong to anybody. And it was an accident. He didn't mind about that. He thought it was one of his own trains. So he said we hadn't to bring the trucks back into the station or the sidings or anywhere near at all, in case they came down again and did crash into his trains. So this morning we're going to put them back on the rails again and invent some brakes for them. Guy says he's thought of something, but we know it won't be any good. We won't do it, anyway, so I hope it isn't."

"Well, I shall know where you are," said Mother. "I don't know where Alice is going, but I expect it's about her fossils again. She took them all off to school yesterday, heaps and heaps of them. You've no idea how she's showed them to me all this week whilst you've been down at the station."

"Well, I *was* moving wood," said Ainsley.

"I didn't think you'd be doing anything wrong," said Mother. "I kept an open mind about what you meant, anyway."

96

"We'll get wood later on," said Ainsley. "There's a lot of drift. Is my dinner ready?"

It was breakfast time now, but Ainsley was thinking of his dinner, because he wanted to be out as soon as possible and back as late as possible. The complete derailment of the whole train of five trucks had put their schedule back, Harold said; but since they had nothing in the schedule it didn't matter much. There is something about train accidents, though, that makes people want to clear them away as soon as possible, even if there is a fine cold drizzle falling all round.

The drizzle was cold, and so was the iron of the trucks. The trucks lay wrecked in their house. The prospect looked worse than it had at the beginning. A week's work seemed to be undone, or worse than undone, because at the end of the first week they had had complete trucks at the end of their work. When the trucks were on the rail this time they would be knocked to pieces.

Bobby picked out a stave of wood and threw it aside. "We'll just have to start and see what happens," he said. "We were all fools to let go. But it can't be helped."

They worked until the midday train had come and gone, and then waited for the clock to strike again, at one o'clock. When it did they stopped, and washed their hands at the station tap. Then they walked out into the South Strand, still in the same drizzle.

"It's got a wretched way of soaking through," said Bobby. "It makes my shirt cling to me, and it's right away down under layers and layers."

"Sort of coldish, too," said Derek.

"It's the small drops," said Guy. "You see, they make you wetter, because they contain more moisture per square inch."

"So do you," said Bobby. "If we want a fire why don't we light it without all this palaver? We've all got matches, I hope. Anybody got a firelighter?"

97

They managed without a firelighter, in spite of the drizzle, but they had to walk a long way down the Strand before they found wood that had kept dry.

"Tell you what," said Harold, after he had tugged at a piece of buried wood in vain, "this is a chunk of metal." He kicked sand aside, and found what they suddenly all expected when they heard of metal: there was another length of rail. There was only a single rail at first, and then they found its pair.

"It points back to where we came from," said Harold. "It'll join. But there's miles of dunes in the way."

He walked up and down, prospecting further, whilst Bobby lit the fire.

"Go on, Harold Harold Harold," said Bobby. "Get some wood, or you don't sit by our fire."

Harold looked up from the railway, and searched for wood. There was a big piece half buried in a dune, but it was too large to move at the moment. Some pieces of drift were very big indeed, trees of the larger size. This one was not tree-size, but it was too firmly embedded. He left it, and found smaller pieces and brought them to the blaze.

They sat on the windy side of the fire and ate their dinners, throwing the paper on to burn as they unwrapped the sandwiches.

"I knew what it would be like," said Bobby, turning his face to heat it evenly.

"So did I," said Harold. "We all smell like puppies, heating up our wet coats."

"No," said Bobby. "I mean we'll just sit here by the fire and forget about the trucks."

"But we can't leave the fire," said Ainsley. "It might go out."

They were arguing about that, particularly with Guy, who said there was a way of keeping the fire in by putting sand on it, which everyone knew was not true, when a stranger's voice asked politely whether they were shipwrecked.

"No," said Ainsley.

"Yes," said Bobby. "Welcome, Man Friday."

The Man Friday he was talking to had walked up to them over the dunes, where he had apparently been gathering drizzle. "I was looking for a gravel pit," he said. "It's not easy to find things in this wilderness; but there was a pit here about the turn of the century, a very rich one, and I'd thought of looking into it."

"It was somewhere about here," said Harold. "The railway ran down to it." Harold was generally quick-witted about this sort of thing.

"Railway?" said the man, looking round him. "I'll find it. Thank you."

"You'll never find it," said Bobby. "It's under the sand. The gravel pit will be under the sand."

"Everything's under the sand," said Ainsley.

"That's a pity," said the man, warming himself at the fire whilst they talked. "The gravel's interesting, and so are the fossils. But if it isn't here, I suppose I'd better make my way into the town. There's another one there I have to visit."

"What for?" said Ainsley. Gravel pits and fossils could only mean Alice. He wanted to know whether there was any question of Alice's coming down on to the Strand.

"Some children have found a fossil," said the man. "It wasn't you, was it? Oh, no, of course it wasn't, I remember now. It was a girls' school."

"We know them," said Bobby. "Shall we take you to the gravel pit? There's a quicker way than going through the town."

"If you aren't doing anything else important," said the man. "I don't quite know where I am. I came off the train, and I thought I might have time for a few minutes down here before going to the other place. I'm just a little bit

99

late as it is. I don't like being late; but what, after all, is half an hour in the life of a fossil?"

They heaped the fire close to itself, so that when it fell it would make hot ash ready to rekindle. Then they led the man along the edge of the sea, northwards, and past the town. No one was about on the beach. They were so alone that a dog, looking over the sea wall, felt it his duty to bark at them.

At the end of the town the cliffs began to rise. They led the man up the end of the cliff, where Ainsley and Bobby had brought the fish back, and on to the path at the top.

"I'll just go ahead and see the coast's clear," said Bobby. "We don't want to be run into by anyone, if you know who I mean."

"We know," said Ainsley. "There's two I don't want to run into."

"I'm brave," said Bobby.

He was back very soon, to say that the coast was just about clear. They escorted the man to the edge of the gravel pit, and paused again to see whether Alice or Miss Palmer had come into sight. They were the two who were absent; but there was a whole gathering of girls in the pit, standing inside their coats in the drizzle.

"Oh, oh, it's her," said Bobby.

"Where?" said Ainsley. "Run like heck."

"Not those two," said Bobby. "That baby one that slimes round me."

"Here she comes, grinning," said Ainsley. "Be polite, Bobby."

"Well I never," said Bobby. "Look at that. She's taken no notice of me. She's gone for him." The man they had led here was getting all the attention of the small girl with plaits who had insisted on showing Bobby her fossils in the High Street.

Then Miss Palmer appeared, followed by Alice. "Blow,"

said Bobby. "We could have mingled with the crowd and not been noticed. And look at him, in the middle of them, and he doesn't remember whether he has to meet male or female, until they're a million years old."

Miss Palmer looked across the gravel pit at them. They turned and went.

They went to the station. All the morning's work had been a plod and a labour, moving broken wood and heaving the solid wheels of the trucks on to the rails. When they left it it had seemed half done. Now, when they came back they saw how near they were to finishing. In half an hour they had the trucks on the line, joined up, and ready to go.

"This time," said Harold, "we'll stick an iron bar through the wheels, and stop them turning."

"Will you?" said Bobby. "Try it, Harold. These wheels are solid, man."

"Now, where did I get that idea?" said Harold. "I was sure that was the way to do it."

In the end they decided to lift the last truck off the rails when they lodged the train. If they put it at an angle it would keep the others still. They began to push, to get the trucks out of the station. They would not move. They had to uncouple them one by one, and test them separately. One of them had a bent axle now, and the wheels could not be moved.

"Four trucks only," said Harold. "We'll use the broken one as a brake. Put it at the end, and carry the jammed wheel."

They loaded the broken truck on to the fourth one of the train. It was easy to do, because the crash had removed all the sides of all the trucks, so that instead of being like prams to push they were like flat carts. The broken wood lay in a heap.

"If we could clear our way through, we could take all that wood to the fire," said Bobby.

"I should think that half the track's buried about ten feet deep," said Harold. "We just came across a bit of it in the hollows. And what about the road? We can't get them over that. There's tarmac over the rails there."

"We could carry them over," said Bobby. "Anyway, it's a level crossing, so they can't stop us. All you need is a man with a flag, and there's only the golf people to stop. I dare stop any of them."

"Or Mr Merriott?" said Ainsley. "He just drives faster if you try to stop him. He's frightened of people."

"Anybody would be frightened of some people," said Bobby, and started a fight. When the fight was over they left the trucks on the slope beside the road, wedged against the broken one, and went across the road, to find where the rails went after they crossed.

They left biscuity footprints in the sand, where the drizzle had crisped the top quarter inch of sand. For a long way there was no sign of rails; and then they struck them again, in a dip, and lost them, and found them where Harold had come across them at dinner time.

"My poor fire," said Bobby, and went to revive it before the drizzle brought it to cold wet dust.

XI

"I wonder what that bloke's doing," said Bobby. "Talking to Alice, I suppose."

"He didn't look like a case of madness," said Ainsley. "He looked quite normal, what I could see. Except for this thing about fossils; but I suppose he was born with a thing about them. Like Alice."

"I wish I was interested in fossils," said Bobby. "Chuck us another bit of wood. There's a serious shortage of fire in this corner of the Strand."

"You could always work up an interest," said Ainsley. "Why don't we work up an interest, if they're all psychological about them?"

Bobby put a stick in the glowing fire, and blew on it, hoping to dry it out and secure some flames. "We did," he said. "It was Miss Palmer who worked it out of me. It wasn't so much the hockey stick, but the sort of her-ness of her. Fancy being like that."

"Alice likes her," said Ainsley. "I've heard her say so."

Bobby said nothing to that. Ainsley went to see what Harold was directing the others to do. They were laying the rails clear along the hollow where they had begun to show. "We should have brought the shovels," said Harold. "If anyone wants to get them."

"You're the one that's doing nothing," said Peter. "I mean, you're the one that isn't doing anything."

"You said that once," said Harold. "What do you mean?"

"He means he's only pretending to work," said Guy. "And you're not even pretending to."

Harold considered what Guy had said. "I believe you're right," he said. "You must have meant something else, though."

They all went back, except Bobby, to fetch shovels. As they went they searched the ground for more rails on or just below the surface. There were appearances here and there, enough for them to follow the line fairly easily, once they knew what they were looking for.

"You know," said Harold, "it doesn't go quite under any dune; not under the middle, anyway. We might be able to dig it out all the way."

"Why do you think we're getting the shovels?" said Peter.

The part that would be worst to do was at the road. The sand had been carved out year after year, to keep the road clear, and thrown to the seaward side, in the hope that what blew off the dune would cross the road and not silt it up at so great a rate. Here there was a long length where no rails could possibly show: they must be far under the sand.

"They might not exist under the road," said Harold. "But we could carry the trucks over, couldn't we?"

"No," said Guy. "There's a right of way. It's a well-known case. A level crossing is a right of way."

Harold thought a level crossing was a right of way for the road, not for the railway; but Guy said that the road had no right of way, because it was a private one, and private roads do not necessarily have a right of way; so, if there was a right of way involved in level crossings, then in this case it must be the railway that had it.

"You were right just now," said Harold. "You might have turned over a new leaf. What's the time? It happened just on the meridian, Guy. All it proves is that no one can tell lies when standing on the Greenwich meridian. That's why they have such a mean time at Greenwich."

They had found already that to move the trucks along the rails there was no need to dig deep. The rails had only to show, and the wheels could find their way, digging themselves in. There was the same noise under their solid metal as there was under the wheels of the engine at the level crossing by the station, when it came to change ends at every journey. There the sand settled again under the first traffic, because there were grooves in the road, where the sand homed itself. Out on the Strand there was nothing to stop the sand from moving sideways and being cleared out of the way.

To dig along the rails was one of those jobs that carries itself on. There was nothing in the sand to make the digging awkward. There was no reason to dig too deep; in fact there was no way of digging too deep. If you ran the shovel along the rail it found its own depth. And there was plenty of space for swinging the shovel when you threw the sand away. Today, too, it was not flying much, because the drizzle had damped the top layer, and the small wind, though it was very cold, did not lift the grains.

They began on the first spur of dune they came to, after leaving the high bank near the road. There was room for two to work at a time. The other three, Peter, Derek and Harold, went on to the next point where the rails showed, and started to dig back.

The work became heavier and heavier. Harold tired of it, rather. He had an idea of himself as general supervisor. He put down his shovel and went to see how the first two were getting on.

"Watch the sweat rise," said Ainsley. "It slows down after the first foot or two, Harold."

"Method," said Harold.

"What we want is a curved blade," said Guy. "Not your method. You get this curved blade, and push it across the top, like a bulldozer, and it moves the sand for you."

"It just moves it on to the part I dug out with the skin of my own teeth," said Harold. "You'll just have to dig on, unless you bring a machine."

"Edwin might think of one," said Ainsley. "But I doubt it. What's Bobby doing, anyway?"

"Housekeeping," said Harold. "I'll go and get him."

Bobby was not sweating any less than the others. He was lying by the fire, certainly, but he was blowing it with his raw breath. "I wish I had some bellows," he said. "I can blow all right, but I haven't any time to breathe."

"You'll get automatic ignition from your face," said Harold. "What you want is some better wood."

"I'm glad I'm not shipwrecked," said Bobby. "Whhhhhh. It won't flame, the flaming thing. If I were shipwrecked, then by the time I'd found some firewood I shouldn't have any fire. It'd be one of the laws of nature for me."

Harold climbed a dune, looking for some sort of small wood that might be dry. There was often a box on the Strand somewhere, ready to be broken up. Bobby had decided, though, to be shipwrecked very far from the beaten track. There was only a heap of bare white twigs, with seaweed dry on it, that had been blown inland by the gale. Harold secured it, shaking off a patch of damp sand, and wondering if the sandhoppers were beginning to waken up. It was surely too early for them to start. When they did appear it was time to be going.

Bobby took the offering and sacrificed it. He made the red centre of the fire larger, and leaned over it, puffing. He was rewarded with a flame. It crept up with his breath as he drew one in, and cast a wreath of smoke into his throat. Tears came to his eyes and his nose ran, and he coughed another heap of ashes up and into his face. The fire had almost beaten him. He had to leave it alone whilst he recovered himself and wiped the dust from his eyes and spat it from his tongue.

When he came back to the fire it was flaming by itself, as if it had never done anything else.

"If you weren't my friend, I would kick you all the way along the Strand," said Bobby.

"What did I do?" said Harold.

"It's the fire I'm talking about. Now we can put some bigger wood on it."

Harold went looking again. He had seen a piece that morning, not far away, and he went for it again.

It was a well-buried piece, lodged in the side of a dune, standing on its end. At first it was immovable in the strongest degree. Harold tugged at it once or twice, and then knew he would have to dig it out. He went for his shovel.

"Can't you find something lying about?" said Bobby.

"There's a bit of ship's timber in that dune," said Harold. "A good thick piece. It only needs excavating."

There was excavating going on along the line too. The four others had worked solidly since Harold left them, and had made cuttings into the sand. There was a look of motorway about this piece of the Strand which Harold had never seen before.

"I know what it is," said Ainsley. "We've dug plenty of holes out here in our time."

"In anybody's time," said Harold.

"But they've always had loose sides," said Ainsley. "This one's got metal edges, so it looks more mechanically minded."

"It's not that," said Guy. "You have to consider perspective."

Harold picked up his shovel and took it away. Ainsley put his into the sand again and threw out another load of sand. There was considerably less distance between the two sets of diggers now. It looked as if joining the two workings would not take a whole day.

Harold went to his own digging and began lifting sand away from the top of the beam.

"It's a boat," he said. "Piece of, I mean. It's blown in upside down, but I'll get it out."

"We're getting hungry," said Bobby. He was still feeding the fire on what they had gathered before. There was enough of that for a camp fire, but nothing like enough for a bonfire.

Harold's shovel scraped in the sand. He uncovered the whole length of his piece of wood. It was longer than he was. He thought it must have been part of the forward end

of a sailing ship, by its curvature. It was always possible, he thought, in a hopeful way, that the rest of the ship was there too. Though it would be useless upside down.

He tired of perching himself on the side of the dune and digging at an angle. He came down to the bottom and dug under the beam, and got his hands under it.

"Come and pull, Bobby," he said. "I can't shift it."

"Get another piece," said Bobby. "I can't leave the patient. It'll get a low temperature. There's acres of wood lying about."

"I'll bring a whole ship in a minute," said Harold.

There was a cheer from the navvies. Their shovels had met on one side of the line. They had immediately been covered again by a fall of sand, but for a moment the line had been clear. It had only been done by leaving serious digging aside, and making the whole job worse through throwing sand where it would have to be moved again, just for the sake of meeting, but it was a sign that the job was not impossible.

Harold thought there might be a hidden joist fastened to the beam, fixed underneath where he could not see it, and going back into the dune. It would account for the immovability. He began to clear behind, from the bottom up. The beam began to stand in a vertical groove, like the ornamental columns on the picture-house in the town.

There was no joist at the back. The beam now hung out of the dune, with only its top curve buried. Harold threw down his shovel and breathed a chestful of air. He took hold of the bottom of the beam, settled his feet deep in the sand, and lifted.

Something moved. There was a tumble of sand from the top of the dune. The beam had shifted. Harold relaxed and took the weight off his hands by lowering them. The beam came down with them, and began settling into the hollow he had made for it. Harold pulled again, and caught the beam very awkwardly too low down. He thought it was about to bed itself down again, and possibly bury itself in a sand-fall. But that was not quite its intention. It settled against the sand at the bottom, but the top of it pulled away. The whole thing came out of balance, and began to topple over.

Harold had no time to let go. He held as tightly as he

could, because all he could try to do now was keep himself from being underneath. The beam hovered, it seemed. Harold thought he must be holding the whole weight upright. Of course, it is easy to hold a post upright: he had seen telegraph poles being kept in place by one man, because all the weight is on the ground, and there is nothing to do except stop the top from getting out of true. He thought he held the beam in that position, for a moment. Then he knew it was not so. It was pressing against him. He let go, and moved away.

He had moved too late. The beam moved with him, faster and faster, and brought him down on his back, thudding into his chest and winding him so that he heard himself bark. The beam lay for a moment with both its ends in the air, with its curve on Harold. Then it fell over on its side, and seemed to dance on his belly.

Harold lay there wondering whether he would ever breathe again. All he could feel of himself was a strangled knot round his heart. Then he could breathe, and in a little while he felt he could move. He would have wriggled out from under the beam, but it was too heavy to move. It weighed more like stone than like wood, and it was beginning to dig in.

"Hey," said Harold. "Bobby."

No one heard. The others could be heard talking and digging. The fire was crackling, the sea was muttering against the beach. Harold lay there with weight gnawing at him and the drizzle filling his face. He spoke again. "Help."

"Just a minute," said Bobby.

"Help," said Harold again. He would have shouted, but he could not concentrate his muscles.

Bobby came walking over, not hurrying until he saw Harold pinned down.

"Can't move," said Harold.

"Are you paralysed?" said Bobby.

"No," said Harold, "it's just this piece of ship trampling on my digestion. Move it, man."

Bobby was standing astride now, with his arms under the beam. He lifted, but nothing happened. "Heavy," he said. "Very heavy. I'll get the others." He shouted for them, and they began to argue that they did not want to leave their successful digging.

"Come and get Harold out," said Bobby. "He's nearly killed himself."

The beam was light work for five people. They lifted it, put it on its two ends, and let it fall the other way. Harold still lay there, taking slow breaths. Then he curled himself up on the damp sand and began to groan, in a relieved way.

"I'm O.K.," he said. "It just hurts. It's getting better, though. I may live."

He lay motionless. They picked him up and carried him to the fire, curled as he was, and laid him in the warmth. He began to relax.

"I've been belted," he said. "Bring the damned thing and fling it on the fire."

They went for it, and carried it to the fire.

"Tell you what," said Harold, "it just caught me along the meridian and the equator. Very vulnerable spot."

Bobby was looking at the beam. The others were holding it, ready to place it where he wanted it. Bobby was puzzled. "Just a minute," he said. He climbed the nearest dune, and looked back over the Strand towards the town. The first lights were going up in the streets, and the afternoon train was coming in. It would wait half an hour and then leave.

"I say," he said. "Do you think we've shrunk?"

"I have," said Harold.

"Not joking," said Bobby. "Do you think we've suddenly got very small indeed, absolutely tiny?"

"You're intoxicated with smoke," said Ainsley. "You've been against the fire too long."

"No," said Bobby. "But that beam: it's not wood; it's just like the most enormous rabbit rib in the world. That's why I wondered if we had shrunk."

XII

Bobby was half-right. Harold had not dug out a piece of wood. His beam was a bone. It was such a large bone that he had not thought it was anything but wood. The four of them holding it now put it on the sand again.

"Better have a post-mortem," said Ainsley. "First, are we the right size?"

"Yes," said Guy. "I'll prove it in a minute."

"Don't bother," said Ainsley. "If it's like most of your proofs we shan't exist at all afterwards. Therefore, we're the right size. Therefore it was the world's largest rabbit. Therefore rabbits are smaller nowadays, therefore that's a fossil rabbit bone, because they were bigger then."

"Fossil?" said Harold. "That's no fossil, that's alive. At least, it kicked like alive."

"Is it bigger than Alice's fossil?" said Bobby. "It must be, of course. Alice could never dig up a thing like that."

"It's not a girl's fossil," said Harold. "That's purely a gent's fossil. Man-size, you know."

"I'm right, though," said Bobby. "It's a rib, isn't it?"

There was no doubt it was a rib. It had the curve of a rib, and one tapered end and one end that had been a joint to the backbone.

"Question is, whose is it?" said Harold. "Ours, I know; but what can we do with it?"

"Send it to Miss Palmer," said Bobby. "What would she do?"

"Alice would like it," said Ainsley. "It would just suit her to have a spare fossil or two. Prehistoric rabbit bones."

Harold stood up now, and held his own ribs. "I feel as if that had been pulled out of me," he said. "Without gas."

They had been going to burn it, if it had been wood.

The fire needed something, so they left the rib for the time being, and gathered wood, whilst there was still plenty of light. Under the cloud that had covered the whole day there was not much light: darkness was settling in early.

Bobby saw the train standing in the station again, and had an idea. "You know that chap who was looking for the gravel pit. Well, he wants fossils. He could tell us what this one is, anyway. He's probably going out on the train. Let's take it along and ask him."

It was a sound idea. It would have been sounder if the rib had been no more than half the size it was. It was one thing to carry it a few yards to the fire, and another to haul it a mile to the station over shifty sand.

They brought it to the siding, because that was the nearest way, and they were gathering their breath again whilst Peter ran ahead to hold the train up. Peter was too late. The signal moved, and the engine snorted. The train came slowly past the siding, and gathered speed down the line.

"Didn't see him in there," said Ainsley. "But he might have been sitting back."

Peter came walking back to them. "I was too late," he said. "I couldn't stop the signal. So we've carried it for nothing. Are you going to show it to Alice? She's in the station."

"Might as well," said Ainsley.

"No," said Bobby. "No, don't waste it on her. I mean, it wouldn't be wasted on her, but if we use it on her, well, we know her already. We could use it better at the Grammar school. We'd have a good excuse for going in then."

"Not until the end of term," said Harold. "I'm not going in there even then, because I'm not leaving then."

"But don't waste it," said Bobby. "Old Alice would only say, 'Thank you very much', tuck it under her arm, and walk away. There's no effect in it."

115

"Wait a minute then," said Ainsley. "I'll just ask Alice whether he's gone."

"Don't tell her anything," said Bobby.

"Doesn't matter if I do," said Ainsley. "She wouldn't believe me, whatever I said."

Alice was crossing the level crossing. Ainsley caught up with her and walked beside her.

"What do you want?" said Alice. "Have you been following us about all day?"

"We haven't followed you an inch," said Ainsley. "Did that fossil chap go on the train?"

"Yes," said Alice.

"Just wondered," said Ainsley. "Good-bye."

He walked away. Alice turned and watched him go back into the station. Then she turned again and went homewards.

Ainsley reported that the man had gone, and that Alice hadn't been pleased to see him at all. "I didn't say anything," he said. "What shall we do with him?"

"Bury him," said Bobby. "Just by the lineside there."

"Dig that rib," said Harold. "I've dug it out enough in its short life of ten million years. Just put it somewhere. No one will pinch it. Dump it in the ruins of the shed."

It was invisible in the wreckage of the shed the trucks had been in. They heaved it over the wall and left it. It settled itself, cracking wood as it went down.

It was time to eat by then. Bobby and Harold had their own food with them. Peter and Guy went into the station office, to drink tea there. Derek went home. He said he was wet enough for the day. Ainsley went home too, although it was only half-past four. The sandwiches had not lasted very long, and there would be food at home.

There was food, and there was Alice too. She and Mother were talking in the kitchen and eating cake.

"Good," said Ainsley, and helped himself.

"Get a cup," said Mother. "What do you think of your famous sister?"

"Nothing," said Ainsley. "What's she famed of?"

"You might have asked me when you saw me," said Alice. "You knew that man was the fossil man. But you don't care. He says my crocodile might be a new kind."

"Named after you?" said Ainsley. "Not so different from the old kind."

Mother put her hand inside Ainsley's pullover. "You're soaked through," she said. "Go up and get in the bath. The water's hot. You aren't fit to be seen in any case."

"Fancy being famous for a little fossil like that," said Ainsley. "It's very small, isn't it?"

"It might be a young one of a kind they know already," said Alice. "Or it might be a new kind of small species."

The next day was Sunday. Ainsley did not go out in the morning, because Dad was busy in the garden and wanted help. Bobby came wandering by, and leaned on the fence a little; but he understood that work was going on, and did not stay. After dinner, when it had settled and lightened, Ainsley went out to see whether anyone was on the Strand. He found Harold at his house, with nothing to do, and walked along with him. They had an idea that the fire might still be alight and perhaps with a little tending could be made to last the week.

"Look, there's Derek and Peter," said Harold. "It's our Strand, really, and they oughtn't to be on it."

But his jealousy was very short. They found that Peter and Derek were picking up wood and making a very good stack of it. No one was very likely to take a pile of wood, no matter how it was made; but they might. To be certain of having it left there it was best to build it neatly. Peter and Derek had made it very firm and square. When Harold found that it had been done for the whole party he helped in turn. The fire had gone quite out. There was a ring of unburnt wood, and some hollow ashes, and that was all. Harold turned over the ashes, looking to see whether the sand had fused into glass. It had not.

"We could move all this," said Peter. "We could get it down into perfect safety if we had those trucks going. But I'm not going to carry it a mile."

"No one intended to," said Harold. "We were going to burn it here, gradually. But we could take it down and sell it. If we've got a railway we might as well use it."

They had not quite got a railway yet, though. They had two ends of it, but the middle was still under sand. They paced along the buried part, or where they thought the buried part was. The line might have gone in all sorts of circles; but they treated it as a straight line. Derek went to the road and stood on the bank opposite the trucks, and the others walked to him from the cleared end, measuring their paces. There was a length of about three hundred yards still covered.

"Looking at it doesn't help," said Harold. "Get digging."

Derek and Peter dug at the edge of the road. Harold and Ainsley started from the other end. Ainsley found the going good. They had the rail to guide them already. The other two had to dig down and find the rail, and they had to lift and carry every shovelful. They carried each one across the road and made their heap there. In half an hour they had made a deep nick in the bank, and the wind was bringing the sand through it and on to the road.

It took them another half-hour to get down to rail level. Every inch forward into the bank meant an avalanche of sand, because there was nothing to hold it back. The nick grew wider and wider, and the job more and more hopeless.

"You know why it is," said Harold. "The sand doesn't lie naturally there. We'll have to put some wood each side of the cutting, or it'll never hold back."

They were standing up the second plank when Mr Merriott's Bentley came to a hushed stop beside them.

"What are you doing?" said Mr Merriott.

"Up here we're digging in the Strand," said Harold. "We aren't harming your road."

"You are," said Mr Merriott. "You are. Look at the sand on it. Why do you think there's a road here at all? Who keeps it clear? Who pays money to have the sand swept away?"

There was no answer needed to the question. Harold was not sure what to say next. It was perfectly true that sand was settling on the road. It was also perfectly true that they could dig on the Strand if they wanted.

"What is this?" said Mr Merriott. "What are those wagons?"

"From the gravel pit," said Harold. "There's an old railway line here. We're digging it out."

"What for?" said Mr Merriott. "Is there any gravel? You have to buy mineral rights if you want to take gravel out of the Strand."

"We're taking wood out," said Ainsley. "We *are* allowed to do that. It only gets left here because it's too far to carry."

"Well, there's no point in digging there," said Mr Merriott. "Those wagons can't cross my road, can they? There's no line across the road, is there? So fill it up again, won't you?"

He wound up the window of the car by pressing a button. Then he drove off, scattering a fair amount of sand himself.

There were other cars using the road, because it was the road to the golf links. No one else stopped.

"I wonder if we're wrong," said Harold. "But we can't find out without looking as if we are. You know what people think. So we'll carry on until we're stopped."

They carried on with the work. There was only one

way to do it, and that was to continue without wondering how much you had done or how much there was still to do.

"I've got to go to church," said Ainsley. "So I have to have tea first."

"What a pity," said Harold. "We could see them coming from here, and you could just go and join them."

"We're not having it in church," said Ainsley. "Mother was saying at dinner time. You'd never guess where it is. You might almost come yourself."

"It's not likely," said Harold.

"It's in the Grammar school assembly place," said Ainsley.

"I won't come even for that," said Harold. "Just you keep a good look out for Miss P. And then you can tell us what the place is like inside."

Alice was very particular that night about Ainsley's appearance. Generally she only told him how miserably disgraceful he was; but tonight she wanted to brush his hair for him and pull his tie straight, and even offered to polish his shoes. Ainsley accepted none of her offers. He came to the service in an independent mood, and stayed in it. Mr Merriott came in rather shyly, and played the piano delicately. It was more suited to him than the harmonium of last week, but there was no way for him to draw out the final notes of each Amen.

After the service Alice wanted to show Mother the fossil. It was in one of the rooms of the school. Ainsley had meant to be taking notice of the whole place, to tell the others; but being with Alice made the eyes of his mind close against new sights. He only smelt that same school smell, and saw the same bars and ropes of a gym. He followed behind Alice and Mother, whilst Dad talked to the vicar and Mr Merriott.

Alice had her fossil in a glass case, and told Mother the interesting points of it. Ainsley looked at it, and then out

of the window. Then he absent-mindedly drew a caterpillar on the board. The caterpillar was the one that turned
into the Headmaster's signature when it was upside down.
Alice came and took the chalk from him and dusted the
board.

"You and your gang have no right in here," she said.
"Get out." Ainsley went, and lost himself in a corridor,
because all the doors from it were exactly alike. He found
his way out before Alice and Mother came from their
examination of bones, and walked home alone.

When Alice came in, his obedience had earned him
nothing. She had spent a long time looking for him in the
school, suspecting him of any sort of trick.

"When I obey her exactly," said Ainsley. "Exactly.
When I obey her very exactly, I still do things wrong. I
give up."

"I bet," said Alice. "It's your fault I don't trust you."

Harold came round on his way home, rather after dark. He came to tell Ainsley that they had cleared the bank by the road right away, down to rail level; and that all there was between the trucks and the best part of the track was the road.

"Tomorrow," he said, "we'll carry the trucks over."

"It's a level crossing," said Ainsley. "We can't wheel everything to the road and then lift it across and carry the trucks. All we have to do is chip out the tar and let the rails out."

"I don't know," said Harold. "Peter's father says the railway was there first, but Mr Merriott's my dad's boss; so it's different for me."

"I'll ask my dad what he thinks," said Ainsley. "He's an independent witness."

"He'd have to be very independent to alter me," said Harold.

Dad was very open-minded about the whole question. He did not come down on either side. "It's a matter of fact," he said. "Mr Merriott's got a road, you've got a railway. I have no idea at all whether you can dig up the road to let the railway through, or whether you can block up the railway to let the road through. One's a private road, and the other's a private railway. Why don't you ask Mr Merriott?"

"He doesn't like us," said Ainsley. "You know he doesn't like people."

"He does," said Mother. "He's frightened of them, that's all. He never wants to offend anyone. If you do anything sudden to him he thinks that his last hour has come. The poor man frets the whole time in case the world is turning against him."

"I'll ask him politely about it," said Ainsley. "And if he says No . . ."

"If he says No he says No," said Dad.

"Christian principles," said Alice.

"Now, don't answer, Ainsley," said Mother. "Or you'll both be at it half the night."

"I'll wait till morning," said Ainsley.

XIII

THE morning was another of those of the everlasting cold spring. The east wind still pushed from the sea, and left twig and tussock without bud and touched with brown decay the leaves of the wallflowers. There was no rising sap in any plant; and there was no moving blood in anyone. At school the Headmaster was perpetually sour now, without any cause in day-by-day events. Harold brought it to mind during break on Monday morning.

"It would be death do part," he said, "if we did the simplest thing. All we've got to do is write Mr Merriott a letter, and sign with the sign of the caterpillar. The trouble is, he'd bring it straight round, and there'd be your little Harold, signed with the sign of the boot."

"It couldn't work, anyway," said Bobby. "Because if he didn't come round, he'd write, sending the permission."

"Refusal," said Ainsley. "It just about seems that we can't ask because it hurts his feelings. It needs an Act of Parliament to give us permission."

"I'm not a member at the moment," said Harold. "But what about a letter from the gravel company?"

"Ah," said Peter. "They're extinct."

"You've heard of fossils," said Harold. "It's the important point, being extinct. It means we can be the gravel pit company, because we've taken over all their things, rails and trucks."

"Spare rib," said Bobby.

"Don't speak of it," said Harold. "I've got a bruise just where I breathe. I told my mum one of you kids kicked me. But what about the level crossing? Somebody write a letter."

It was difficult to decide who the letter was to be from.

It was one thing to become the gravel company; it was another to find what it had been called. They had to leave it over until they came out of school and went down to the station again. There Peter looked about until he found a notice that had once stood by the sidings. It warned trespassers to keep off, and was signed: "(By Order) K. Wilstead, Propr. South Strand Gravel and Aggregate."

"What's aggregate?" said Derek, when he had read it once or twice.

"Aggregate means 'and company'," said Guy. "It's a lot of things put together." He was right in some sort of way, but no one took his explanations as fact in any case.

"We won't take any chances," said Harold. "Just head the letter with it as it is."

"It isn't an address," said Bobby, who was getting the job of inscribing the letter. "It isn't of a place."

They gave the address, in the end, as the station. There the letter stopped for the time being.

"You lot write it," said Peter. "I'll go out and dig." Derek and Guy went with him. They were sitting in the waiting-room of the station, where there was a fire. They had never been in there before, and had not suspected a fire at all. Peter had known. For a long time he had used the room to play in, which put off passengers who might have thought of waiting.

"Dear sir," said Bobby. "This company is desirous of reopening the railway . . . the light railway . . . that runs across your road at . . . Where does it run, Ainsley?"

"Just near the meridian," said Ainsley.

"Just to the south of this station," said Harold. "In accordance with . . . What are we in accordance with?"

"Free speech and co-education," said Bobby.

"In accordance with bye-laws of this company," said Harold. "You see, I've just proclaimed a bye-law, so it's in accordance with that. In accordance, blah blah, we are about to run trains up and down the City Road, in and out the Eagle, or words to that effect, signed Bobby Hutchinson, Secretary."

"O.K.," said Bobby. "I'll just copy it out clean." He bent his head over the job. "How do you spell 'eagle'?" he said.

"Fool," said Harold. "Don't put that bit about the City Road. Put something about the Strand."

"It's done," said Bobby. "Now where shall I put it?"

"In Mr Merriott's letter-box," said Harold. "Let's read it first."

He read it, and Ainsley read it. They both came to the conclusion that dictating was all very well, but seemed to make you leave out what you had intended to say. "Put it in a PS.," said Harold. "PS., is this all right with you?"

Bobby borrowed Peter's bike, and went off down the road with the letter in an envelope borrowed from the station. "It's been cheap," said Harold. "We might have had to borrow a stamp as well."

With the secretarial work done they went back to digging. Bobby returned with the bicycle, not having seen Mr Merriott. He had put the letter in at the door, and now they had to see what happened.

Peter was full of complaints about having his bicycle borrowed, so Bobby and Ainsley buried it under a heap of sand from the workings, and left it to fossilize at its leisure. Peter had to look for it very much later on, he said the next day, and only found it by putting his foot through the spokes of the front wheel.

Peter's father was a little puzzled when they went to his office in the afternoon. He knew nothing of the letter they had written, so he had studied the outside of the answer they got to it all day, wondering what to do to a letter to no one, because it was still a private letter and not his concern.

Peter went in and took it from him, and his father was glad to lose the responsibility. He had found it delivered

126

by hand when he came in the morning. All he had thought of doing was putting a stamp on it and posting it at the post box in the station, to see whether the Post Office would know what to do.

"You open it, because you're being secretary," said Harold to Bobby.

"I hereby declare you opened," said Bobby, putting his thumb under the flap. "Easy, isn't it?"

"Read it," said Harold. "You're not Little Jack Horner, sticking in his thumb."

" 'Dear sir,' " read Bobby. " 'I regret I cannot allow you to expose the rails under the road to my house. Yours faithfully, N. Merriott.' "

"I wonder what he means, exactly," said Harold, looking slyly at Ainsley, to see whether he appreciated the joke.

"We could say we thought it meant something else," said Ainsley. "But it would be a waste of a good lie."

"We should have let Guy read it," said Bobby. "He could make it mean anything."

They went out to see what Guy could make it into. Guy read it, and without any prompting he decided that to regret you cannot allow something means you are sorry that the thing isn't being done, and therefore if anyone wanted to do it they would be welcome.

"You must be right," said Harold. "We ought to have made you do it in the beginning."

"We caught ourselves," said Bobby. "Who would dare to explain that we mean what Guy means?"

"We'll have to carry them over," said Harold. "Oh, my ribs. They do ache."

Bobby was ready to try one of the trucks. He and Ainsley undid the coupling of the one nearest the road. All the trucks were still standing there, with the broken one at the lower end of the slope, holding the others still. The two of them could move the truck slowly up the rails, to the edge of the road, but they were not able to lift it the inch and a half on to the tarmac. Peter and Derek came to a wheel each, and with one at each corner they had it off the rail and on to the road. They pushed it across the road.

It did not go very easily. It was now running on the narrow flanges of the wheels, and the flanges dug into the tarmac. The tarmac itself was little more than sand and tar. The flanges cut their way in and made a very noticeable mark.

"He'll think we've dug it up," said Harold. "Take it off the road at once. We'll have to tell him it would be better to use the rails. We know where they are."

It was perfectly easy to see the rail under the road. Once you knew it was there it was hard to miss, though you would not suspect it unless you had followed the rail along. It was easiest to feel it by hand, a smooth ridge like a vein on the road. The mark left by the truck was a nasty gash in comparison, as if a knife had been slashed across and it had healed up badly. In the end, to save the road, they had lifted the truck back where it came from.

They were still there, looking at the place, when Mr Merriott himself came by. He slowed up, and looked down at the road. He saw the marks; but he was not going to stop just then. He looked at the marks, and then at each of them in turn, and drove on, looking angry and affronted.

"Made a friend," said Harold. "I wish we hadn't tried."

"It's his tar," said Ainsley. "It isn't his road. I mean, it was here before, wasn't it, but he put the tar on."

"That's right," said Harold. "It's the tar he's worried about. It's very expensive."

"Is it?" said Peter. "We've got a drum of it at the station, and we just use it for patching holes if they get too bad. It isn't very expensive."

"It's putting it on that costs such a lot," said Harold.

There was nothing to be done about the crossing now. They went on into the dunes and dug out another fifty feet of track before it was time for tea. Then they walked back to the town along the edge of the sea, with the little flat-edged waves teasing their ankles.

The next day Harold thought they should try the other owners of the road, the Golf Club, to see whether anyone there understood how necessary level crossings were to railways. There was only one difficulty there, and they discovered that whilst they were thinking about another letter. The Headmaster was a committee member of the Club, and at the moment his temper was so sour that they were certain he would never agree to anything they suggested. It was only with reluctance that he would agree at present that anything was right. He would have argued about 1066 if that had been their period of History, or about twice two, if he had taken them for Arithmetic. The whole school was wary of him just now. Even Bobby did not run along the High Street.

The Golf Club had best be left severely alone. Mr Merriott was the only authority they could go to; and they had been once.

"But fair's fair," said Harold. "We only did go once. We ought to go three times, and the one that wins twice is the winner. There are rules, after all."

No one felt like going to Mr Merriott. The others thought that Ainsley ought to go this time, through knowing him in church. Bobby had tried once, and it was someone else's turn.

Ainsley began to have an idea about it. He thought he should have something to argue with. The trouble was that Alice ought to be consulted about it. But he would sort that out later. "I'll do it," he said. "But I may not live through it. Alice may kill me."

He laid in wait for Mr Merriott that evening, by the station. He jumped out when the car came quietly round the corner, and waved to it to stop. Mr Merriott looked all round, and stopped a yard or two away, so that Ainsley had to go to him.

"What have you done?" said Mr Merriott. "Blocked the road with your games?"

"Oh, no," said Ainsley. Then he added "sir," to make Mr Merriott more agreeable.

"What, then?" said Mr Merriott.

Ainsley ordered his thoughts for a moment. Without taking a great deal of care he could get into a muddle. In fact, he could any moment be telling an enormous lie. "It's my sister, sir," he said. "She's found a fossil, you know, and it's a new kind, and she might have to give it a name."

"What's that to do with me?" said Mr Merriott.

"Well, sir," said Ainsley, "it would be nice if she could give it your name."

"Would it?" said Mr Merriott. "What's it the fossil of?"

Ainsley kept his mouth closed. He had to think of a way round saying "crocodile" straight out.

"Did she ask you to ask me about it?" said Mr Merriott.

"It was going to be an exchange for the level crossing," said Ainsley.

"You're an impertinent youth," said Mr Merriott, "I'm sorry to say. I don't feel at all flattered at being asked to share my name with a crocodile. Yes, I read my paper, so I know about it. In fact, I seem to know more about it than

130

you. And you know about the level crossing." The car window went up electrically, and the car moved off silently.

"Well," said Harold, coming out of the station. "Did it work?"

"No, thank goodness," said Ainsley. "I was mad to try it. I offered to name Alice's fossil after him. Alice would have killed me."

"She'd have named you after something," said Bobby. "Poor Alice. You are foul to her, Ainsley."

"She wasn't here," said Ainsley. "But I bet she gets to know."

"So he wouldn't do it at all," said Harold.

"Said I was impertinent," said Ainsley. "Was I?"

"No," said Harold.

The time had come to decide what to do. Bobby had the opinion that they had been unduly polite, and that they need not have asked Mr Merriott anything. Harold wanted to agree, but he did not want to be tangled up with Mr Merriott at all. Ainsley thought that they had done their best, and what they couldn't win by bargaining they could win by taking. The feeling of the meeting was that it was time to dig the level crossing out of the road, and cross it when they wanted. If Mr Merriott wanted to stop them he could do it afterwards.

"It'll upset him," said Ainsley. "My mother says that anything like that makes him miserable."

"Not all that miserable," said Harold.

"I wouldn't like to be miserable," said Bobby. "I remember before I got to know you lot of layabouts that I was dreadfully frightened of you. I thought you would put frogs down my neck. I was very frightened of that. I used to make Edwin put them down, to practise me. But you never did it. I thought you might be against me, you see. But now you do much worse things than frogs to me, but I don't mind at all."

131

"I wasn't going to put a frog down Mr Merriott's neck," said Harold. "Or yours."

"I don't know what I mean," said Bobby. "But I think we should make the level crossing, and I think we should send Mr Merriott a letter telling him we're going to, and he'll know who it was and he won't think an enemy did it."

"If I went into my room and somebody had turned out all my pockets and drawers and cupboard I would go mad with the world," said Ainsley. "But if the person left a note saying he'd done it, then I wouldn't mind so much, even if it was Alice."

The clock struck five then, and they went out on to the Strand to do some plain digging, whilst they thought over Bobby's idea. Harold gradually came through to seeing what he meant; though it was a thing that did not trouble him. He would never think the world was against him, even if he might think he was against the world. He did not see how it could have any effect on anyone, except to warn them in time for them to stop what was planned.

"Right," he said, when they could see no more on the Strand. "Bobby, you be secretary again, and write another letter. But you can make it up yourself this time. The only thing is, we won't tell him when we're going to do it."

XIV

THE crossing was made on Monday night. Before that, though, there were certain arrangements to make, as well as the letter to Mr Merriott. Ainsley thought it would be best not to let Mr Merriott have a letter on Saturday, to stop him from easily talking to Dad or Mother on Sunday. Since they did not want to touch the road without warning, they waited over a good and dry week-end into a squally Monday.

There was a little practice to do, as well. Harold thought they should have dummy runs, to ensure that everything went smoothly on the night. It was the dummy runs that were not at all successful. They mostly consisted of Harold bent over his watch, reading it by match light and saying: "If we allow three minutes for this, and four for the next piece, we ought to be all right." It was one thing to have the time in mind, but Harold insisted on seeing the times through. They had to sit through blank minutes, waiting for Harold's watch to say they had finished.

"It's like watching a television before it's switched on," said Bobby. "Possible, but not likely. No one ever does it."

There was something they could practise with success, though. Since they were going to take up some of the road's surface, they thought they should replace it later. Peter rolled out a small drum of tar from its place in the station, and they pulled out the rag-wrapped stopper in the end of it and looked in. The tar was solid with cold. They poked a stick down to it and tried to break the surface and release the runny part underneath.

"Very difficult to stir," said Bobby. "Get a longer spoon, Peter."

"That's not how it's done," said Peter. "You use a shovel."

"I guessed that as soon as I saw a hole two inches across," said Bobby. "Just shovel-sized."

"Put a fire under it," said Ainsley. He had not really considered it at all, so he was surprised to find he was right. Somehow the idea of tar in a barrel meant tar that was runny all the time, unless the surface dried. They rolled the barrel along the rails into the Strand, and put a fire against it. In a little while there was the lung-opening smell of tar, and the barrel became sticky to touch. Then it began to steam inside, so that it was impossible to see what was happening. Bobby put a stick in, and brought it out dripping and shiny. He sprinkled sand in it, and the end of the stick became a specimen of road surface, which he handed round for inspection.

They took the barrel from the fire and buried it in sand, to cool and be hidden. The smell of tar lingered, until they could no longer smell it. Their noses were used to it.

Harold experimented on the road itself. They had to see what sort of job they would have in taking the tar up over the rails. To stop comment they dug out a little strip some distance away from the level crossing, using a cold chisel.

"The toffee's not quite hard enough," said Harold. "It sticks to the chisel but it comes away. I'll just have to calculate how long it'll take."

On Sunday night they took a subscription of a halfpenny each, and bought six stamps from the machine at the Post Office.

"Dear sir," wrote Bobby. "We intend shortly to replace our level crossing over your road. Yours faithfully, R. Hutchinson, Secretary."

"He'll get it in the morning," said Harold. "If we're alive at nightfall, then we'll go and see to it. We'll arrange it in the morning."

Bobby licked the flap of the envelope. "Shall I drop it in the box?" he said. "All agreed?"

The letter tumbled down into the pillar-box. "That's big business," said Guy. "That's how fortunes are made." No one knew what he meant.

Harold was thoughtful in the morning, without much to say. He kept his progress up to time on the way to school. Ainsley and Bobby walked behind him.

"He's being the brave leader," said Bobby. "Thinking about our future."

"We don't have a leader," said Ainsley. "We're not a gang, are we?"

"We shall be if we don't keep him back a bit," said Bobby. "He's just beginning to give orders, don't you think?"

"He can always obey them himself," said Ainsley. "I'm not supposed to belong to any gangs, only to be with friends."

Harold was not giving orders, but any operation has to have a plan, and any plan a planner. He was the planner, and he had to nurse them through the right actions. Straight after school he took Bobby and Ainsley out on the Strand, and helped them make a sunken fireplace, because they would have to have a fire for the tar, not far from the crossing, and it would be best if the fire did not show in the dark. They brought up the barrel of tar from its underground hollow, and set it in the fireplace and put the fire ready round it. They did it as early as they could, hid their work as much as possible, and left the Strand.

"I don't think anyone saw us," said Harold. "If they did we've gone home now. We'll come out about nine o'clock and do the job itself."

"Nine o'clock?" said Ainsley. "I bet Alice hears me getting out of the window. She would."

"Get out of the door," said Harold. "I shall."

Ainsley had often been out of the window at night during the summer. They had not gone on the Strand then, because of the sandhoppers, but roamed the woods, trying to catch rabbits. Mother had known perfectly well that he had gone out, and had never minded until he had come back late one night after dark. She had waited for him, at the window, and said only, "You must always be in by nightfall." Ainsley could not see how summer could equal winter in any way. The night was fallen by the time he went to bed in winter. He thought it would be fair to resolve to return by half-past ten, which was much the same thing as summer twilight. He thought about it for ten minutes just before tea, until Mother said he must be worrying about something. He said he wasn't, and proved it to himself by thinking no more about it. He had his plan for going decided.

He went to bed at nine, and straight out of the window. He left it open after him, so that he would make no noise when he came back. He stepped on to the coal-house roof, and down the wall at the back, and was out in the road the next minute.

He had a feeling that this would be one of those times when no one else turns up. He turned his face to the night wind and walked down to the station. There was the day's last train standing there, and a few people in the station. It was not yet late and distant night, but only evening. The train said "Hof", and then nothing for a moment, then went off into the night abruptly, laughing smokily. The station lights went out, first on the platform, then in the office.

Ainsley came out across the yard, and the yard light went out above him, leaving only the glimmer of the pilot jet. Ainsley stopped, waiting for someone else to come.

There was a flicker of light out on the Strand. He walked towards it along the road. His footsteps sounded louder than the rest of the world put together. He left the hard and walked in the soft of the sand. It was all ankle work, in the dark, like walking on a nearly solid sea in a swell. The sand undulated below his feet and made the stars overhead seem to pitch and wander.

There was a smell of tar. The light he had seen was the glow of the fire. Harold had come out early and set it going.

Ainsley whistled two notes, to let Harold know he was coming. The fire disappeared from view at once. Silence set in. Ainsley felt all at once that perhaps Harold had been caught by Mr Merriott, or some other authority—the Headmaster, perhaps—and was now tied up, waiting like a bait for the rest of them.

A light touched his face. Ainsley stood still. There is no way of telling who is beyond a torch.

"It's him," said Bobby's voice. "You take over until the next one comes, Ainsley."

"Take over what?" said Ainsley.

"Sentry," said Bobby. "We've got to keep a look-out, you know. We might have to run like heck."

Peter had been following Ainsley, and took over sentry duty almost at once. The first person he stopped was Bobby, who had been there all the evening. The second he arrested was Harold, who had been there since darkness fell.

"You're too good," said Harold. "Just watch out for lights approaching. No one from the other side will come without a light. Just watch for lights."

Peter next tried to arrest Flamborough lighthouse, which winked at him from twenty miles away. Harold set him to watch the fire and see the tar didn't boil over. Derek and Guy then came up quietly and overpowered Peter, and dragged him to Harold. No one had seen them arrive.

"No sentry," said Guy. "That's how the geese captured Rome."

"That's how you captured the goose," said Harold. "Are we all here?"

He gave out his plan. Two watchers were to stand on the bank, one looking north and one south. The others were to dig out the rails under the road, one at each end of each rail, working towards the middle. In case of interruption they were to scatter in all directions, and go home. He did not think it would be safe to try to win any sort of battle of wits against anyone in the dark.

The noise of the chisels was frighteningly loud. It

seemed as if it would be audible all the way to the town in one direction and all the way to Mr Merriott's house in the other.

"Stop," said Harold. "I didn't think of that. It's the hammers on the chisels."

"Oh," said Bobby. "It doesn't make so much noise if you put your thumb in the way."

"Put a handkerchief over the chisel," said Harold. "Does it make any difference?"

"It aches just as much," said Bobby.

"Get on," said Harold. "I couldn't afford new batteries. Those are all I had."

He had provided them with a torch each. There was a yellow glow from them, and they illuminated the road awkwardly. It was better when the first three inches of groove had been cut at the edge, because then the torch could be laid in the trench and would shine automatically in the right direction.

The work went on slowly. They found that wrapping the head of the chisel in handkerchiefs was clumsy. It was easier to wrap the hammers. Shreds of handkerchief began to fall round the work.

One side was finished, and then the other. Harold used a shovel to gather the dug-out tarry pebbles together and put them aside. They would have to be put back. They stopped work entirely for a moment, and listened in all directions. There was no one to be heard or seen.

The next action was moving the trucks. By daylight the

noise of them was bearable. By night, working secretly, the row they made was tremendous. Not only did the wheels ring as they moved, but new squeaks had been set up. The couplings jangled like steel necklaces, and the frames that held the axles exhibited every kind of rattling looseness.

"They'll be out now," said Bobby. "They'll think we're stealing a scrap-yard."

"Do it all at once," said Harold. "If we take one at once they'll get used to the sound and gradually come to us. Go over in one, and they'll never focus. Put your lights out. We'll do it by feel."

It took all six of them to move the train. By the time they had the trucks moving they were too full of their own physical movement to be able to think of the noise of metal. Puffing and panting is nothing from a distance, but when it is in your own head it drowns other sounds.

The trucks moved grudgingly. They had settled in their places.

"It's uphill again," said Harold. "They want to go down the hill again."

The last truck, the broken one, was loaded on to its neighbour. Two of them had to do that, tipping it up and heaving it on to its back. It fell with a hollow thunder, and its good pair of wheels shook in their bearings and squealed. The rest of the train grew heavier. The incline was pulling at them.

Six pairs of hands set them moving, slowly at first, then a little faster. They got them moving by repeated jerks, making the next impulse come before the impetus of the last one had died away. In a little while the train was moving almost by itself; a gentle hand on it led it along, but the hand had to be firm as well as gentle.

There was no room in the narrow cutting beyond the road for them to stand beside the trucks. As the trucks crossed they vanished into the shadow of the bank, and in

140

the end they were all pushing on the last truck. The first crossing had been made.

"Two of you get the tar," said Harold. "The rest of us can block the trucks in here."

There was a certain amount of competition to bring the tar. There was suddenly less as each person found how hot the steel barrel was. They brought it in the end with the claws of two hammers under the flat strap of handle. It was put down by the road.

Meanwhile the trucks had been immobilized in the usual way, by putting the broken one down behind them. The four good ones leaned against it and drove its wheels deeper into the sand.

Harold took charge of the tar. He tipped the barrel and poured out a black stream into the groove they had just emptied. It ran along, and they helped it with sticks. They brought the chippings they had excavated and dropped them in and trod them down with their heels. Harold slopped on another coating of tar, and they smoothed it with a flat edge of driftwood, and scattered sand on it. By torchlight there was not much to see now, though there was something. They put down more sand.

"Not very convincing," said Bobby. "It's like a false moustache."

"Can't make it perfect," said Harold. "Leave it alone, and it'll grow right."

Next they covered the track on the station side, brushing sand over it. Harold took off his coat and flapped it over the newly laid sand and the old, well-trodden sand at the side, and reduced the surface to a uniformity, though it was not like any surrounding part of the dunes. After that they brought wood and covered over the cutting where the trucks were. There was plenty of wood in the pile they had made, enough to lay two ways, so that it would hold sand up. When the roof was on they heaped sand over it, and tidied out their marks on either side. At the edge of the road they made the bank look as much like its old self as they could. They put the barrel of tar in the narrow cave with the trucks, buried the sunken fire, and walked home along the road.

It was quarter past ten. Ainsley climbed his wall silently, stepped in at the window, saw that his hands were quite covered with tar, and the soles of his shoes were thick with sand, and put his pyjamas on. He put the window down, and opened the bedroom door. The television was on downstairs. He went to the bathroom and washed the tar off his hands with Alice's shampoo, putting it on before wetting his hands. He swilled the greyness off the basin, and went to bed.

XV

In the morning Harold did not appear, nor did Bobby. Ainsley slipped away from Alice and waited in the usual place, rubbing his cheek where the keen air was getting at it. He waited as long as he dared, and then walked on alone. He was a little worried about the other two. He began to construct an attitude, in case he needed one when last night's events came to notice. Had the marks on the road been found already? Were Harold and Bobby so soon caught by authority? Ainsley wondered which authority he feared most. He thought the Headmaster was the one that made him cringe. In a way he had the most power, all day; and he had a determined way of carrying out what he had promised. But Mr Merriott would not go to the school. He did not associate any of them with school. He would go home. Perhaps he had already gone to Bobby and Harold.

Ainsley walked along briskly, not daring to run in the street. It was just as well he didn't, he thought in a little while, because a car was keeping pace with him. He could see its bonnet just at shoulder level. He walked on, taking no obvious notice. In a little while he would cross the road, and look right over the top of the car, and ignore the driver, because it would be the Headmaster. He would take great care of traffic drill.

Then the car moved on. It was not the Headmaster's car at all. It was a police car, with two policemen in it. Ainsley stopped where he was. They had never thought of the police. Yet here they were tracking him. That was where Bobby and Harold were, arrested and being questioned, imprisoned, tried. In spite of his good resolution Ainsley crossed the road without looking. A car braked beside him, and he heard a window being wound down.

This was the Headmaster's car. Ainsley moved along the pavement, using the Grammar school girls as if they were trees and he were a fugitive in a wood. The Headmaster drove on.

There was no air of anything unusual at school. There was the same formless bustle of people in passage and room. But there was no sign yet of any of the others. Ainsley sat at his desk and waited.

They all came in together. They did not look as if they had been arrested, or as if they had anything on their minds at all.

"What have you done to your face?" said Bobby. "Walk into a tree or something?"

Ainsley felt his cheek again. It was still smarting gently. "I got tar on it," he said. "They saw it this morning and scrubbed it off. I washed my hands last night, but I didn't think of my face."

"We went up to have a look at the crossing," said Harold. "It looks as if a tank had been across it seven or eight times. It's sure to be noticed."

"I thought you'd been arrested," said Ainsley. "There was a police car in the High Street. It trailed me."

"Police?" said Bobby. "He wouldn't. Did we do anything police-ish?"

"We'll find out," said Harold. "I'm sure we didn't. I didn't think of police at all. There hadn't been any up at the crossing, or we'd have seen their footprints."

The bell rang for assembly, and there was no time for further examining of consciences.

The day went by, and nothing grave happened. The day was an ordinary day, with no extremes from anyone. The school clock ticked round its measure of hours, and the lessons slipped away, until the last one was through and it was time to go.

They went to the Strand. "If they want to arrest us, they can do it there," said Harold. "We don't deny it, do we?"

"All guilty," said Guy. "You get time off for pleading guilty."

"You get time off for not being guilty," said Harold. "It's not the same thing."

The Strand was empty. No one else was moving anywhere in sight. They walked along the road, and came to the unmistakable double scar across it, like two very bad welds. The afternoon train hissed in the station, and then moved off, with steam blowing coldly amongst its wheels.

"I wish we'd been caught doing it," said Ainsley. "Then we would know what to expect."

They had not much longer to wait. There was a movement by the station, and Mr Merriott's car came on to the private road, and moved quietly along to them. It stopped. Mr Merriott got out, and stood by the radiator of it. He did not like to go far from shelter. At first he said nothing. The six boys looked at him with their different expressions. Harold was ready to explain; Bobby was going to explain in a way that defended them; Ainsley wanted to know what was to happen; Guy was searching his mind for something he had read or heard that would apply to the situation; Peter was wondering what the affair had to do with Mr Merriott—he had not gathered that it was Mr Merriott's road; Derek wondered what he would say if he had to speak.

Mr Merriott was wondering what to say as well. In the end he did not open his remarks with speech. Instead he tapped the road with his foot.

"It's . . ." said Harold and Bobby together.

"Sir," said Ainsley.

"Not occur again," said Mr Merriott quietly. When he had spoken the words he found it easier to go on. "Not the Gravel Company. This is a private road. This is my road. You have no right. No right at all. Why you think you can dig . . ." He left his sentence unfinished, because to finish it with the words "It is beyond me to understand", which were what he had thought of, was not true. He thought he would understand it if people who were not so rich began to hate him. He was very conscious of being rich, and on the whole he enjoyed it, but it gave his conscience something to worry about as well.

Harold did not explain anything. There was no need to, because everything was understood.

"Not any more," said Mr Merriott. "I know you all. I know your fathers. That's where I'll go." He turned away and got back into the car and drove on.

Ainsley looked at Harold. "We shouldn't have done it," he said. "It frightens him. He thinks we might turn on him like a rabble in a crowd with guillotines."

"He can always stop being rich," said Harold. "I could help him there."

The moment had passed, though. Mr Merriott was going to do nothing this time; the trucks were across the road, and the new gravel company had won its fight. The only thing to spoil it was that there had been no need of a fight: they could have carried the trucks across without bothering anyone.

"I tell you something," said Bobby. "All that wood we made into that big pile. Well, it's here, just as far as we can get it without crossing the road. Well, what did we get the trucks for?"

"To bring it here," said Harold. "Of course."

"And who brought it here, in the end?" said Bobby. "We did, with our own hands. You and me."

"It's all right," said Harold. "Why worry? We've got plenty of tar left. We've spoilt the road, haven't we? We can't make it worse. All we have to do is dig it out again when we want to drive the trucks over, and fill it again."

"Brilliant," said Bobby. "He'd never know."

"I only just thought of it," said Harold. "Now let's have a bonfire in celebration."

146

They started a fire where they had had one before, about a mile along the Strand. The way to it was not clear of sand yet, but they brought the trucks out as far as they could, moving them out of their shelter one at a time, because of their weight and the difficulty of getting a hand to them with so many people to help. The shovels were with the trucks, so the train moved on slowly, with its engineers finding the line ahead as they went.

The line still ran uphill. It was difficult to understand why and how, when the general effect of the Strand was one of flatness: that is, the dunes rose up all over, but the ground they stood on seemed to be about the same height above the sea in every place. It would be a difficult thing to measure.

"It would be so that the full trucks went down alone," said Ainsley. "The horse would only pull up empty ones. Isn't that right?"

"It's the principle of relativity," said Guy. "One piece is relatively higher than the other, and one thing is relatively heavier than the other."

"I wish you hadn't learnt to read," said Harold. "I know everything you say is wrong but I can't prove it."

The fire that Bobby had just made became neglected, and fell down into furry ash. Bobby came to dig, because the block on the line seemed short enough to be taken up before dark. With six people digging, the line cleared almost as they watched, and they were able to bring the trucks right up to the most distant point they had found.

"On, on," said Harold, throwing down his spade and sitting by the fire.

Like Harold they stopped for breath, and then looked at the biggest obstacle so far. It was a full-grown dune, about fifteen feet high, as big as a house. The rails ran straight into it.

"We'll have to move the lot," said Harold. "You can't get straight sides on this stuff. You know sand has to slope.

We'd better start at the top and work down, then we won't have to lift the sand up."

"After you, Capting," said Bobby.

Harold climbed the dune. Sand tumbled round his feet, bringing them down half the distance he took them up. It takes more steps than the distance indicates to climb a dune. The others went up after him, and they stood in a circle at the top.

"Don't send any down on the line," said Harold. "Just put it out to the sides. Beware of fossils, too. This is the dune where I found mine."

Harold found again, with his first plunge of shovel. It struck something hard. He dropped it and dug with his hands. He was not the only one. Ainsley on one side of him and Guy on the other found something hard too, and cleared with their hands a place on the slope.

They uncovered a knobbed rank of bones, and out of the bones grew more, sloping down the dune just under the surface. They worked the sand downwards, where it went easily, and in two or three minutes had uncovered part of an enormous backbone and three huge ribs hung from it. In the end they slid down the dune and looked at what they had exposed. The dune looked like the side of an elephant now, with the ribs showing grey against the sand.

"Is it breathing?" said Harold.

"Shut up," said Bobby.

"Isn't it a strange feeling?" said Harold. "Let's find the rest."

They all abandoned shovels and took to hand digging, and followed the line of the backbone, three going one way and three the other.

Ainsley was going headwards. The backbone sloped down and went farther into the dune. He got his spade and followed it. It meant slicing out a great hollow in the sand but none of it had to be lifted, and it flowed away

148

from him downhill. He cleared another segment of the back, and found a rounded bone of a different sort.

"Headbone this end," he said. "Right in deep."

The head seemed more important than the tail. The others came to look, and began to dig. They had to clear a huge part of the dune away, and every grain, after a time, had to be moved twice. The inside diggers threw it back, and the outside ones hurled it away.

"Never mind about the railway," said Harold. "We can scrape that clean in a minute. We might find a fortune of ivory in here. Look out for tusks."

The sand grew more solid and wet. It was only the surface that was completely dry in almost any weather. The middle of the dune dried out each year, gradually. Now it was of a dampness that almost held the grains together.

They saw a big dome of skull under a cliff of sand; but the next movement of the shovel covered it again. Each time they saw it it was longer until they saw it again, because more and more sand came down.

It began to grow dark. Harold felt in his pocket for one of the torches they had used the night before, but he had not brought one. Bobby went back to the fire and put wood on it, to breed a flame. When he had a heart in the fire he took up a shovelful and brought it to the excavation.

"Don't put it down," said Harold. "Just hold it, or we'll kill it with sand."

Bobby held it up as a torch, and fed it with small wood. Then the damp sand seemed to hold itself in a cliff above the skull. Ainsley, as its discoverer, smoothed sand off the bone.

"Any tusks?" said Harold, indicating them in the air from his own jaw.

"No," said Ainsley. He was scraping away with his hands, more or less in the dark. He could feel the shape of the thing under his hands. There was the round bone of the braincase, and then a long projection, running

150

straight forward. He followed it, tunnelling into the sand
with his finger-tips, scratching as he went. Sand forced
itself under his nails and roughened their backs. His arm
went as far as he could push it, and still he was not at the
end. He dug downwards now, drawing his hand back
along the tunnel he had made. He dug shapes he could
not see with his eyes or his mind. He dug until he was
well down in sand and had put his arm under the bone.
Then he called for light. "I think there's a lot of stones
here," he said.

Bobby brought the light nearer. Ainsley had not felt
stones. He had been digging along the side of a huge jaw,
and in the jaw were teeth seven inches tall and as big
round as the top of a Wellington boot. There was a row of
them, glittering white along the tunnel he had made.

"Not an elephant," he said. "It's a crocodile. About
fifty times as big as Alice's. Won't she be raving?"

XVI

ALICE was getting ready for one of her big rages when Ainsley got home. In a way they were a relief, because in the end of them she usually hit Ainsley with something, which didn't hurt him, but made her sorry she had done it, and civil for quite a long time afterwards. When he came she got up and came close to him and sniffed.

"He never washes it," she said. "It smells of seaweed. He never brushes it either, so I suppose it doesn't matter." She went back to the fireside where she was sitting.

"What?" said Ainsley. "My hair?"

"Yes," said Alice. "It must have been you that used my shampoo; but I don't see how, when you haven't even washed your hair."

"I never wash it," said Ainsley. "I just let wind and weather keep it clean."

"I must have used it myself," said Alice. "But I'm sure I didn't. I would remember a thing like that."

Ainsley sat down for his tea. If Alice had asked him he would have confessed to using the shampoo as tar remover; but now he let her fume to herself.

Before they left the Strand they had firmly resolved not to say anything about the crocodile to anyone. Bobby had wanted to call Alice in as an adviser, but the votes had gone against him. Everybody else, except Ainsley, wanted to think a little longer. Ainsley wanted Alice to have nothing to do with it; but he had no objection to asking some of the other girls what they thought. The trouble was, if they came, then so would Alice. As one who had discovered with his own hand the long jaw and tremendous teeth, Ainsley felt he ought to keep separate from Alice as a finder of crocodiles. It was a pity that Harold had really been the first finder of a bone: it would have been interesting to have two people in one family to name two crocodiles after.

In the morning Harold was glimmering with an idea. It came into crystal form in the High Street, and he had to stop opposite the Grammar school gates to think it out. Ainsley and Bobby stayed with him, because a thinker needs support, and because they could watch the girls going in.

"Got it," said Harold. "I'll tell you after school. It's nearly clear in my mind."

"Stay as long as you like," said Bobby. "We're comfortable."

"Behind schedule," said Harold, looking at his watch. "I wonder if we could do another short cut."

"Oh, no," said Ainsley, and took Harold's arm. Bobby took the other, and they dragged him away.

"Look out," said Harold. "Here comes the old man." The Headmaster was crawling past in his car, on the lookout, they thought, for rowdy behaviour.

"I bet he's got a sort of radar in that old crate," said Bobby. "The speed-limit kind. He ought to feel flattered that anyone wants to hurry to his establishment."

"I don't suppose he does, when he sees who's arrived," said Harold. "Us, I mean. Would you like to be him? Would you?"

After school they went up to yesterday's abandoned digging. The sand had dried out and fallen again, so that almost all the exposed bone was covered again. Anyone casually walking by would not easily think that any digging at all had been done there, the fall had smoothed the outline so.

"Still here," said Ainsley, putting his hand into the dune and caressing the huge teeth. "What shall we do?"

"Dig it out," said Harold.

"We know that," said Bobby. "It's a natural temptation to dig it out. What shall we do with it later?"

153

"Keep it all in one piece," said Harold. "Then we'll take it away."

"Where?" said Bobby. "I don't think even Edwin would let me take that home."

Derek thought they could paint it with luminous paint and put it at the edge of the sea, and drive everyone out of their wits. Guy thought they should orientate it; but since he meant articulate he had to do a lot of explaining, with Harold asking him which way it should point.

"Actually," said Harold, "it's not a bad idea. But it's joined up already, so we don't need to. You wouldn't be much good, Guy, if you weren't joined up."

"I don't think he is," said Bobby.

Peter thought there might be a danger from dogs. He had some thought of packs of them coming and worrying any bone they found.

"Not fossils," said Harold. "There's no scent left in fossils."

"There is in coal," said Peter. "That's fossil."

The first thing was to dig it out. Whatever they wanted to do with it, it would have to be out. Like the railway, there was only one way to do it: go on working until it was done.

"But what a job," said Bobby, looking up at the overtopping dune. He forgot that yesterday they had started to move the same dune for another purpose. "I know it's interesting," he said. "But it's not all that interesting. Couldn't we invite the girls to dig it out?"

"Not Alice," said Ainsley.

"Ah, that's the point," said Harold. "If we dug it out, then we could show it to the girls. Can't we take it down to the Grammar school and show it to them? They'd be bound to let us in. We wouldn't let them see it unless they did let us in."

"We've got a railway, right up to its very face," said

Bobby. "It's welcoming little engines in with gently smiling jaws."

"Poor Bobby," said Harold. "But you're right about the railway. You see, I've got this general sort of idea, but I'm not sure how to end it up. We don't want that Miss Palmer getting in the way of our romantic associations. It's such a big thing."

"Anyone in their senses would have discovered a baby one," said Bobby. "Then we could have put it somewhere and invited them to it, if we knew their names. But this thing, it's about as private as the middle of the High Street."

They had not stopped digging whilst they talked. One party was working at the tail end, and the other at the head. As they went deeper the work became worse. At first the sand needed to be moved only once. Then it had to be moved twice, then three times; and after that there was no knowing how often it had to be lifted and thrown farther away. By the end of the day there was a whole range of bones showing, and the top was off the dune; but there was another dune growing beside the first.

When the light began to fail, and they started to knock the bones by accident, they stopped the main work and concentrated on the sand already moved into the second dune, carrying it away as far as they reasonably could.

"This is only the top of the dune," said Harold. "The top is much smaller than the rest. There's nine times as much in the bottom half as there is in the top."

"I wish Guy had said that," said Bobby, wiping a sandy hand on a sandy forehead. "I'd have taken it better."

"The thing about pyramids," said Ainsley, "is that they build the bottom bit first, so when they were half-way through they only had a tenth of it to do. If you see what I mean."

They had no need of a fire tonight. They were glad to

stand in the cool wind every now and then as they worked, and glad to walk back home by the water's edge and trail their feet in the waves. Ainsley dabbled his hands in the water to take away the grittiness, and found the salt water stinging a burst blister.

The next night was the same sort of labour; but by now there was beginning to be some sort of progress and order in everything. The bones were no longer merely showing through the sand. The ones along the back were sticking up out of it, and were actually able to cast shadows when a finger of sunlight wandered in from the sea. The diggers had started the afternoon's work high up and able to see the town. By the time they came down from it the town was out of sight, and all round was only sand. Ainsley was used to having nothing but sand round him: it was a state he could achieve any day of the year; but now, with the prehistoric feeling of the bones edging his mind, he could imagine himself having slid back to the prehistoric times himself. Just for a moment he might have been the slayer of the crocodile, and the rest of them the tribe gathered to strip the flesh away. Then Ainsley moved his feet, and the springy flesh changed to yielding sand, and the horizon of time gone to the boundaries of today.

"Big old basket, isn't he?" said Peter. "Wonder who taught him to walk."

The next day the work was even slower. There seemed to be no progress made at all. They worked from four o'clock until seven, and were all the time paddling about in newly moved sand. It spread wider and wider, and did not seem to uncover any bones they did not already know. When dark came on them again Harold said, "We've been going on like a lot of layabouts, I think."

"It's blooming depressing," said Bobby. "Toil, toil, toil. What are we doing it for, I'd like to know. The girls would be quite excited to see it as it is. If they want the rest, then let them have it. There's more of them."

"There's plenty of blokes in school," said Harold. "Why not get them?"

"It's our crocodile," said Bobby. "If they came they'd overcrowd us."

"Well, I thought it out," said Harold. "But we'll still have to dig it up. Man, you've hardly started yet. We won't say anything to the girls, not a word."

"Who made you give orders?" said Ainsley. "You behave the laws, Harold."

"Listen," said Harold. "We don't tell them anything. We get him up, load him on the trucks, and run him down to the Grammar school, put him in the yard, and stand him up neatly, with our compliments."

Ainsley thought that would be a hollow action. What was there in it to introduce them to the scholars of the school?

"I know what happens then," said Bobby. "We get told to come and take it away, and we have to bury it again. I know, I've had some."

"Ah," said Harold. "That wasn't a genuine fossil, hall-marked in every bone, was it?"

"It half was," said Bobby.

"It won't do anything for us," said Ainsley. "It'll bring Alice round our necks. We've done it once already."

Bobby thought again, and agreed that a real fossil was a proper and kind present; and that such a big one was sure to be an adornment. "But things have been fool-proof before," he said. "Except when we were the fools."

"Saturday night," said Harold. "That's the time to do it, the day after tomorrow."

Ainsley surveyed the shapeless mound they had made of the dune. Its outline could be seen in the darkening, and it seemed to be as large as ever. He said that they could never do it. So far, he said, they had not taken out a single bone, apart from the one that fell on Harold, and that was obviously a loose one and probably belonged to a different

157

crocodile. "What if it's half a mile long? What if it is the Loch Ness Monster?"

"A man who saw it proved it didn't exist," said Guy. "So it won't be that."

"Well," said Harold, "I'll have to do it all myself. Who found it? Whose is it?"

"Nobody's arguing about that," said Bobby. "You found it, you keep it."

"Right," said Harold. "I'm going home now. But I'm

coming out first thing in the morning, and I'm going to stay here all day, until I get the thing out. If you don't want to help, well, it doesn't matter. The girls will be pleased."

"Skip school?" said Bobby. "Why not? That makes it into a sensible proposition. I'll help you in that case."

Ainsley was bound to offer himself then; and the others agreed one by one. The next day was a Friday, and by the time they were missed they would be back again. No one worried very much about people who missed Friday and came back on Monday with a slight cough. Six coughs were as easy as one.

"That's fixed," said Harold. "We'll just have to manage about food and stuff. Bread and water will do."

Ainsley found better than bread and water at home. There was a whole cake forgotten in a tin, and a can of corned beef, and a bottle of ice-cream soda that belonged to him by rights in any case. It really needed ice-cream to

make it drinkable, but things like that are merely detail to thirsty people.

The day was fresh as ever, with the same east wind blowing cold out of Europe; but there was light high cloud, and there might be sunshine. Ainsley walked carefully beside Alice, not rattling the bottle and beaker in his satchel. Then he dropped behind in the usual way, and waited for Harold or Bobby.

They came at the usual time, and walked down to the

top of the High Street at the same time as always. This was Harold's calculation. It was necessary to come so far, to avoid one master or another. Here it was necessary to avoid the Headmaster, who came along at rather variable times. They had to wait until he was past before going out towards the station, along a road that had no cover or hiding-place.

They stood in a shop doorway, and watched the Headmaster's car go by. They gave him time to get right through the High Street, and walked out to the station.

Guy and Derek were out at the site before them, and were standing in the cool wind saying they would never get warm. Peter came up when he saw that all the rest had arrived. It had taken him some time to remember that morning that they were not for some reason going to school when they should.

Harold arranged an orderly method of digging. At first he did none himself, but walked about the showing bones making marks on them with red paint, using a very small brush that was usually his best one, and reserved for picking out bright parts on model aeroplanes.

"Why mark it?" said Bobby. "Isn't it a lump?"

"I don't think so," said Harold. "The very first bit wasn't. I think all the rest will fall apart when we start moving it, so we want to know how to set it up again. Look at all these enormous back bones. They're all just alike, so you can't tell from looking at them what's what."

When he had painted he dug with the rest. Now and then he would stop and go round to find newly exposed bone, and mark that.

Peter worked along the tail, and came to the end of it. He went on for a yard until he was convinced, and then stopped for a rest, and the others followed his example. They sat among the bones. Ainsley leaned against a rib. By now they had hollowed out the animal's chest, so that there was a bridge of spine supported by the cage of ribs.

No one had gone inside, but there was a gap where
Harold's rib had fallen away, and Guy had shovelled from
there. Ainsley leaned, and the rib shifted. He leapt up,
thinking it might land on him; but it had shifted the other
way. Now he had upset it, and the whole skeleton fell
apart. The farther ribs went out of balance and tipped
over, uprooting themselves. Those on the seaward side,
where Ainsley was, leaned inwards, and the arch of ver-
tebrae dropped in its separate fragments on to the sand, as
heavily as stone.

"Busted," said Derek, moved from silence by the
catastrophe.

"Just what we wanted," said Harold. "You don't think
we could have moved it in one piece, do you? Why do you
think I marked it?"

"Thought it was your name," said Peter. "I generally
write my name."

XVII

THE collapse of the skeleton brought them almost to the end of their digging. At first they had thought it tiresome to have to move all the bones before they could dig any more, but when they had moved each one they found there was very little more to do.

They laid the pieces of backbone out in order on the sand. Each piece was very heavy; not quite so heavy as stone, but not much less. They manhandled the ribs to a position beside the spine. Harold's numbers were the only things that helped them now. Without them they would have laid the bones in a heap in no order at all.

"There should be some legs," said Harold. "But hyenas may have got them when it had just died."

They dug for legs, and found a heap of bones. Harold had no numbers for them, so they laid them out in the best order they could. Giving each leg two joints, knee and ankle, they had bones enough for eight legs.

"People aren't made like that," said Bobby. "They're much more complicated. Those bones will just have to go in a heap, the same as they were. All the animals with a lot of legs don't have any bones at all."

"Lobsters and spiders don't have bones," said Harold. "You're quite right. And then there's snails and slugs; they don't have bones or legs."

"Or skulls," said Bobby.

The skull was the last piece they had to move. It was so obvious and unlike anything else that Harold had not bothered to mark it. It went at the thick end of the backbone, and it was impossible to make a mistake.

It was impossible to move the skull, too. It was too heavy. It was like rock, and seemed to be bonded to the

162

earth. They could not shake it or make it tremble. It lay there grinning openly with its long jaw.

"What a face it has," said Bobby. "It's about eleven feet long." He had been pacing along it, four strides from end to end of the skull.

"It wouldn't go in my bedroom," said Ainsley. "It's ten foot six by ten foot six."

"You could get it in cornerwise," said Harold. "But how are we going to move him anywhere?"

They tried again, but it was like trying to lift a railway engine, completely ineffective. Somehow no one thinks of bones having any weight: your own are so light, or even without heaviness at all, considered as lumber. Their useful effect overcomes their weight.

"Lever it with a piece of wood," said Bobby. "One under it, and one under that." He brought two spars that had been laid ready for the fire. One he laid alongside the skull, and the other he thrust under it and over the first, to give it something to hinge on. They put their weight on the lever.

The skull sat there as smug as ever. The wood groaned and bowed, then cracked smartly up the middle, so that they all let go at once. The wood leapt into the air and danced on one end, then dropped flat on the sand. They could hear its stresses being relieved for some time after that.

"It's against being moved," said Harold. "I'm not going to try that again. We've got to get it on a railway truck, and that's that. How could we do it?"

Ainsley had seen a film on television, in which a very large stone was lifted fifteen feet in the air a quarter of an inch at a time, by putting lengths of wood under it and not letting it fall back into place when each sweating millimetre was gained. But that, of course, only lifted things up. It didn't take them along, and the skull would have to be taken along to the trucks.

"It wants a machine," he said.

163

"That's what I've been thinking," said Bobby. "Let's go down and see Edwin. Is it his dinner time, Harold?"

"It's everybody's," said Harold. "We'd better not all go down in the town. I'll go with you, Bobby. You others stop here. Don't let him get away."

They were gone half an hour, and when they came back they were riding in a break-down truck, with Edwin driving and all four wheels spitting up sand from the ridged tread.

"What's the situation?" said Edwin. "My God, have you been having a barbecue? What a heap of chop bones."

"They're all right," said Ainsley. "It's this we can't shift." He patted the skull on its cranium.

"What is it?" said Edwin. "Petrol-dactyl or whatever they call it? Too big."

"Crocodile," said Ainsley. "But don't you tell Alice. She's got one already."

"Only a little one," said Edwin. "Well, here's some chains. Get them round the thick part of your friend's bonce, and we'll have a go. Where do you want it taken?"

"Just on to one of those trucks," said Harold. "If you can do it."

"Sure thing," said Edwin. "Just get him lashed up. I haven't got too long."

They tunnelled right under the skull and led the chains through the hole. Edwin came to see they were safely lodged and would not slip off.

"You'll damage it," he said. "That's bone, isn't it? The chain will crush into it. You'd better put something round the chain."

They took off their blazers and packed them between the chain and the skull. Edwin backed the truck up to the place, and let the hook of the crane down.

"You lot get hold of the beak end," he said. "Stop it swinging about. It'll want to clout the back of the truck when we get it up. I'll wind the thing up."

164

Edwin could wind the geared crank of the jib with one hand, and lift the front of a thirty-two-seater coach. The lift was very gradual. This was merely a bone, he said. He thought it was a pretty big one, and might weigh a ton. He ran in the slack of the chain, and began to take the weight. The others stood by the snout of the creature, and waited for it to swing free.

It was a long time before it left the ground. By the time it did Edwin was turning the crank very slowly with both hands and getting warm. The breakdown truck settled on its springs so much that the back tyres touched the mudguard.

"Lot of wind and no lift," said Edwin. "You want an ambulance for that thing. I don't think I can lift it with this. You want a builder, not a mechanic."

He turned the crank again, and the skull suddenly lost its immobility. It moved and began to swing towards the truck.

"Hold it," said Edwin. "It'll smash the truck."

They could not hold it entirely. They felt they were slowing its swing, but they could not stop it. Edwin let it down to the ground again. The truck rose off its tyres.

"It's no good," said Edwin. "It weighs four times as much as I thought. I can't lift it with this. You'll have to drag it."

"It'd scrape to pieces," said Bobby. "All that way."

"All what way?" said Edwin. "Where are you going to put it in the end?"

"No comment," said Harold. "Could we make a sledge for it, do you think? Would that do it?"

"Hurry then," said Edwin. "I've got another half-hour. Can you do it in that time?"

They thought they could make something, until they came to look at their wood. There was nothing that Edwin thought strong enough; and no two pieces were alike.

Peter said there was a pile of sleepers down at the station, and a telegraph pole that had been left behind because it was broken across the middle, though not separated. The Post Office engineers had toppled it on to the rails when they replaced it, and cracked it severely. Edwin unhooked the chains and went down to see what he could borrow. Peter did not go with him when he was reminded he was at school.

Edwin came thundering back a quarter of an hour later with the telegraph pole in two pieces laid on the deck of the truck, and a dozen sleepers stacked behind the cab. He got up and tipped them on to the sand.

He took over as adviser now. Under his instruction they put half of the sleepers at intervals under the skull, digging out more tunnels underneath to do so, making a hollow irregular deck for the load. Then they lifted each sleeper in turn and propped it up so that they all stood at the same level. Under the ends they rolled half the pole, and took out the props, letting the sleepers down on the pole. They did one side and then the other, and made of it a very large sledge.

Edwin put the chains on the towbar, and clamped them on the ends of the pole. He started the truck, and put it in gear, with all four wheels driving. The sledge moved. It was held together with its own weight. Edwin pulled it out from the edge of the dune into the level space between two more. He stopped moving, and backed up a little way, to slacken the chains.

"Now," he said, "we'll put the rest of the sleepers in and give it a solid shelf to stand on, and all you have to do is bolt it down, and it'll never fall to pieces."

"We can't drill holes in a fossil," said Bobby. "What would Alice say?"

"Fasten the sleepers to the poles," said Edwin. "I'm off now. What are you going to move it with in the end? This truck again?"

"We'll have to," said Bobby. "You come after dark, and we'll shift it secretly."

"Tonight then," said Edwin. "I'd take it down there now, but it might fall to pieces on the way, and there isn't time to go slowly."

"You can't go in there today," said Bobby. "Not where we want to put it."

"Besides," said Harold, "we haven't thought out every detail yet."

"See you," said Edwin. "Feed your friend up a bit. There's no flesh on him at all."

The next thing to do was load the rest of the bones on to the railway trucks. They laid the pieces of backbone on like drums, and pinned them down with ribs. The four trucks did not mind the weight being piled on to them. The only thing they had to watch was the height of the load, because it might topple when they moved. They would certainly have to make two journeys for them, because the four trucks were very small compared with the load.

"We'll move it after dark," said Harold. "Just take up our tarring and nip across, and be out of Mr Merriott's way before he knows anything about it. We shan't be more than half an hour at the road altogether, considering we're going down the hill this time."

Bobby pointed out that they would have to unload the trucks at the station, and then push them up the hill, and almost a mile to the remaining bones, load up again, and cross the road a third time on the way to the station. He thought it would take them two hours, even in daylight.

"We'll lash everything on with some wire and take them in one," said Harold. "The wire's in my blazer pocket. Where's my blazer?"

All their blazers were still under the skull, making a soft bed for it. They could pull at sleeve or collar, and even reach the pockets Harold wanted to reach, but they could not pull the blazers out and wear them.

"We'll get them out tonight," said Harold. "When we unload the headbone."

Until then they strapped the rest of the bones on to the trucks. Peter had to have Harold on his shoulders, and Derek held Bobby, because the heaps of bone were so high.

"Safe enough, though," said Harold, "if we go gently."

The next thing was the question of bolting the sleepers to the poles the sledge ran on. Edwin had thought of that when they put the poles under the sleepers, and had lined the existing holes up so that the poles were under them. All they had to do was drive some sort of spike through. Peter thought of the obvious thing: the spikes that had once been in the same holes in the sleepers. There was a pile of them in the station, pulled out and cast aside, and a sledgehammer that would drive them.

Fetching them took longer than fixing them. The holes were there already in the sleepers, and they only had to hit them in. There was no need for great care, because they could not bend the spikes like nails.

"That's it," said Harold. "I'll just put two or three extras in at the front to fix the chains to. It's these little details that make all the difference."

Darkness and hunger came together, and an extra coldness of the wind. They put their raincoats on, and went home.

"Back here in an hour," said Harold.

"Meet at the station," said Bobby. "And come here together. I'll bring Edwin along."

They went homewards slowly, because they moved the trainload of bones with them, as far as they thought was safe: not quite to the edge of the road. They left it well back, so that car headlights would not pick out the grey whiteness towering up into the dark.

Ainsley found it odd to be in the bright lights of home, after being centuries away in the Strand. Most of the day he had forgotten about the actualities of domestic affairs. He sat by the fire and watched tea being made ready.

"You look as if you'd been playing games all day," said Mother. "Red-faced and out-of-doorish."

"We have been out of doors," said Ainsley. He wanted badly to confess where he had been; but Alice was there. What he did was nothing to do with her. He could have told Mother, but only if she had held it a secret too. He had a feeling there would be an inquiry on Monday: too many people had been away at once. Still, it was no time to speak now. He had to put the thought away from him and eat his tea.

"You'd think he was some sort of germ, the way he engulfs his food," said Alice. "He doesn't eat it, he wraps himself round it."

169

"I remember a little girl who had to be washed after every meal," said Mother.

"Home life," said Alice. "It's like a cartoon."

After tea Ainsley said he was going to see Harold.

"Don't get into mischief," said Mother. She was not really thinking what she said, so Ainsley took no notice. "I don't know what time I'll be back," he said.

"I do," said Mother, attending better. "Ten, and no later."

"O.K.," said Ainsley.

They gathered at the station, crowding into the office. Mr Knight was still there, waiting for the last train to come in and leave. All the day's heat was still gathered in the room, curling the papers on the desk and thickening the window with dew.

Edwin stopped in the yard with the truck, and pipped his hooter. They went out blinking and gasping at the cold air, and climbed on to the truck.

"Hold tight," said Edwin. "We're leaving the road now."

They were not long on the desert road. In a little while the massive skull was looking back at them with its shadows. Edwin left the headlamps on, and checked over the bolts they had put in. He brought the rattling chains and fastened them to Harold's extra bolts and to the first three sleepers. "Spread the load," he said. "Now where do you want it?"

"In the yard of the Grammar school," said Harold. "We've got it all worked out. I went in and got the key, and we don't need to go into the High Street at all."

XVIII

"You're joking, of course," said Edwin, jerking the chains to see that they were firm.

"Man, no," said Bobby. "We've got to express ourselves, haven't we?"

"I don't know," said Edwin. "Have you?"

"Come on," said Bobby, "you said you would. And you don't need to go in the High Street."

"No one will see you," said Harold. "It's the back gate, you know, behind the market-place."

"I know," said Edwin. "I was just wondering what you were up to. Are you sure it isn't hooliganism?"

"Not this time," said Bobby. "We hooliganed before, and buried a dead fish in their gravel pit. This is to make up. I mean, we don't want the thing, do we?"

"There's nothing *wrong* with it," said Edwin. "It just might be awkward if we were caught at it."

"Put a tail light on it," said Harold. "Or head light, whichever you think suits it best."

"That part's all right," said Edwin. "No law against dragging sledges. If you wanted to dump it in your own school yard, well, I wouldn't mind. But the Grammar school's different."

"It's a rag," said Ainsley. "Isn't it a rag?"

Edwin nodded. He had wanted to have a reasonable explanation for his own mind. Putting the bones in the Grammar school yard was a rag, because no harm was done to anybody or anything, no one was involved in any expense against their will, and the deed had an air of strangeness about it.

"You lot walk," he said. "One of you go up in the back and tell me if anything goes wrong. Which way do you want me to go, Harold?"

171

"Round the back streets," said Harold. "Have you got anything to cover him up with? We don't want people looking at him as we go."

They had nothing for a cover at the moment. Edwin started the engine and began to move slowly. The heavy sledge sat sullen and obstinate on the sand whilst the chains tightened and bit into the wood. They could hear it cracking under the iron. Then the sand under it creaked in turn, and the sledge began to move. It left two furrows six inches deep, and flattened the sand between. A bow wave built up ahead of it. They watched the wave with their torches. The sand was flowing like a liquid, rising and falling as the ground ahead fell or rose. The truck and its tow left a broad track, with tyre patterns at either side, fringing the two ditches and the tableland between. Along the tableland, spoiling it, came Bobby, keeping an eye on the end of the crocodile's snout.

They came down to the station. The sledge came out higher than before, on to the level tarmac. Now it left a brown mark as it rubbed itself away on the bound gravel of the station yard.

Edwin stopped outside the station, came round to look at the skull, and then went to borrow a tarpaulin and a tail light, both of which could readily be found in stations. He came back carrying the red lamp and dragging the tarpaulin.

"Somebody will have to sit at the back holding the light," he said. "There's nothing to fix it on. Let's get going."

Peter and Ainsley sat on the back of the sledge. Peter had felt he ought to be in charge of the railway's lamp, and Ainsley felt he ought to be in charge of Peter.

The town was very quiet. It was about nine o'clock of a cold night, so the streets were naturally empty. It was certainly a cold night. Ainsley's fingers were beginning to die on him, losing their movement and turning white. He put

172

his hands over the lamp to gather the warm light rising on the wick. The red but chill glow of the domed lens shone back at them from walls and from the road itself.

They went a long way round, Ainsley thought. Harold was in the cab with Edwin, telling him where he ought to be. Then they were at the top of the market-place. The Grammar school was ahead, and there was a road running across their path. They would have to cross the road before passing through the gate of the school.

The cab door banged. Harold had got down. Ainsley heard his footsteps crossing the road. Then there was a rattling of doors and the shaking of a bolt. The truck moved again, and in a moment they were under the arch, and Harold was putting the leaves of the door over again.

The engine of the truck drummed in the narrow passage, and its smoke lay wreathed on the air. Harold locked the door, and turned to come back. His face was red in the red light.

Edwin moved on, and they were in the large open yard of the school. "Where?" said Edwin.

"Across there," said Harold, indicating a wall without a door. "Turn round first."

Edwin made a large circle and brought the sledge close against the wall, backed up a bit, and switched off.

There was silence round about, and empty buildings, cold air and a feeling of something done with a great effort.

They unveiled the skull. It looked larger than it had on the Strand. Ainsley turned the red lantern on it, and it seemed as big as a small car.

"Get it off the sledge," said Edwin. "Take those sleepers back, they're not ours."

At first they could see no way of getting the sledge out, without knocking it to pieces, and it began to seem impossible to do that. Edwin managed to loosen two bolts with a tyre lever, and they were able to draw out one of the sleepers that happened to have no skull resting on it. In the gap that was left they put a jack, and jacked the skull up clear of that part of the sledge. They propped it with two blocks and the sleeper, took out a second sleeper from the sledge, and lifted the other end of the skull. They were then able to pull the sledge apart and take it away, leaving the skull standing for the moment on two pieces of wood.

"That'll fall on someone," said Edwin. "Best get it on the ground." They did their best to take the remaining sleepers out, but it was not possible. All they could do was lay them flat, not propped up on blocks.

Harold was busy with the sledge. Edwin came to help him pull it entirely apart and heap it on the truck.

"Give up," said Harold. "We'll want this. There's all the rest of the bones, ribs and things. They've got to come. We can't get them any other way unless we carry them one by one."

"Do that small thing," said Edwin. "I'm not coming in here again. A rag is a rag, and they wear out, you know."

"O.K.," said Harold. "But you saw those ribs. Do you think we can get them here without being seen?"

"Stop involving me," said Edwin. "I've helped you once."

"I suppose you'll have to help us again," said Bobby.

"Just once then," said Edwin, giving in again. "And I'm not coming in here any more. We haven't got out the first time yet."

They were out for the first time two minutes later, with the sledge behind the truck. Edwin thought it was very unsafe, because they had not dared bang the spikes back in again in case they were heard. They stopped under a street light and hit them with a hammer, and settled them before going on to the station. Edwin had to go there to return the tarpaulin.

They had rescued their blazers from under the skull, and put them on without being able to examine them,

174

except for finding their names inside the collars. They looked at them in the station, and checked on the damage. There was a great deal. There was so much sudden new wear that if it had all happened to one blazer there would be nothing of it left. Ainsley had a sleeve with a hole beaten in it. It was not cut, but crushed out of existence. Peter's was scored down the back, and Harold's had had the buttons punched clean through the cloth.

"Moth and rust doth correct," said Guy, looking in vain for the last six inches of his left sleeve.

Edwin wanted to know where the next load was. They told him it still had to be collected from the Strand, and that they had only to wheel it down the railway to the shed.

"I'll wait for you," said Edwin. "I'm not doing any road-breaking. I don't know anything about that."

"Only just everything," said Harold. "By the sound of it."

They went to the Strand without resting at all. Ainsley's shoulders were begining to ache. He had been using them all day, since nine in the morning. Even Harold was losing the desire to be exact.

"We'll just belt the train across," he said, "and tidy the road up some other time. Those chisels are up in the bank beside the crossing, and the four hammers. I can't be bothered to light a fire and melt tar and all that. It's half-past nine already. We've had a twelve-hour day."

They were hurrying now, and kept no look-out at all. Four of them dug out the rails at the crossing. They let the pebbles scatter themselves, and then threw down hammers and chisels and went to get the trucks.

The trucks were so heavy now that the axles did not easily turn. They did not know that that was what stopped a load of such a weight running away irrevocably. As it was they had to push to get it moving at all.

The cutting was the worst part. They could have gone

175

up on the bank and pushed against the load, but the load was barely safe as it was. They all had to go to the back and lean against the tail of the fourth truck. The broken one had been cast aside, because they had no spare power to move it with as they came along.

"We ought to have put out one sentry," said Harold. "You'd think Edwin would do that at least."

"We're nearly across, I think," said Ainsley. "Just starting on to the road, anyway."

"Lights," said Bobby. They shone their torches on him, but he was not asking for light. He had seen the loom of headlights turning to a distinct fan. They were coming from the south, where Mr Merriott lived.

"Push harder, boys," said Harold.

They pushed harder. The train moved out on to the road. The first truck was half-way across when pushing was no more use. The train stopped.

They scrambled up the bank and down again on to the road. They looked first at the rails, and found the trouble. There was a carelessly left pebble lodged in the cleared groove, and a wheel had half-climbed it and then jammed it hard against its own flange.

"Chisel," said Harold. "Where are the chisels?"

They were all under the trucks, which was the last place they had looked. Harold took one and began battering at the pebble.

"Push the trucks back," he said. "I can't shift it."

The car was coming nearer. The beams were brushing the sky. Then they touched the top of the bones, perforating the heap. The car had reached them. The lights dipped, and shone lower.

"Clobbered," said Harold. Bobby expressed the same idea in different words. Harold spoke up. "We shan't be a moment, Mr Merriott."

Mr Merriott blew his horn very loudly. Harold got up from where he had been hammering, throwing his tools

176

down. "Ready," he said. "Let's be off." He put his hands up to the load in front and put his weight on it.

"Grave case . . ." said Bobby, but he had no time to finish his remark. The load began to sway; there was a crepitation of bones, and they shifted; they shook, and began to cascade, falling off the truck on either side. Harold jumped back, and a piece of backbone rolled over the growing heap of bone, and brought him down.

The rumble of moving bone ceased. There was silence, except for the murmur of Mr Merriott's car engine, and the sea stroking the beach.

Mr Merriott got out of the car, and stood in the dark behind his headlamps. "I said," he said, "I said you were not to do it. I told you. This time I shall tell your fathers. This time you have gone too far. I warned you."

"Don't say anything," said Ainsley. "Just get this lot out of the way."

With six of them to help the bones were dragged aside

177

quite soon; but of course any wait is a long one to a motor-ist, and Mr Merriott paced about, impatient.

Then the track was clear, and they were able to move the train across the road. They were in trouble again there, because they had covered the rails with sand, and that had to be moved by hand. For safety they blocked the truck wheels with a rib before going back to the road to clear that. For the moment they pulled everything to one side, to make room for the car.

"What is this nonsense?" said Mr Merriott. "Why can't you move wood at a sensible time of day? Why do you have to break up my road to get it? Believe me, I shall be at your houses the first thing on Monday morning. Some things need punishment, you understand. I shall ask for punish-ment."

Then he had gone. The car went down to the town, and out of sight.

"He'll worry," said Ainsley. "He'll be sorry he was angry, and that'll make him worse on Monday."

"We've got plenty to worry about on Monday without that," said Bobby. "I've got a feeling we shall have to emigrate, or leave the country at least."

"It's my fault," said Harold. "I'm not taking enough care. We should have rehearsed it. But we'd better get a move on now, or Edwin will have gone for ever."

"Bones," said Bobby. "It's a dog's life."

XIX

Ainsley looked in to the sitting-room on his way through the house to bed. "Good night," he said.

Mother looked up at the clock; but Ainsley had gone. He got into bed, and heard Mother coming upstairs. By the time she opened his bedroom door he was asleep, and when he woke in the morning he still expected her to be finishing her walk up to his room. Whilst he had been calculating how many steps there were left, sleep had swept up on him.

He was very hungry. He heard Alice's alarm ring. It was quarter to eight. He sat up in a sudden panic that she would be going to school before he remembered it was Saturday. The sitting up made him hungry, so he got up. Alice had throttled the alarm and begun to move about her room.

Mother was laying the breakfast table. "Funny thing last night," she said. "Weren't you coming in at ten?"

"Ish," said Ainsley. "Ten-ish."

"Oh, ish," said Mother. "That will account for the sort of vision I had of you at eleven, coming into the house and going up to bed. By the time I got to you, you looked as if you'd been asleep since six. You were quite switched off."

"I always go to sleep about then," said Ainsley.

"I meant ten o'clock," said Mother. "Next time, eh?"

"It was things," said Ainsley. "Things."

It had been things. It had been unloading the trucks and loading the sledge three times, and three trips round the streets that were growing quieter and quieter, so that the roar of the breakdown wagon's engine and the dragging of the sledge had been louder and louder to the listening ear. But no one had seen a bone. In the end, after being worked

179

on by everybody else, Edwin had driven the truck three more times into the Grammar school yard, fearful each time that there would be someone waiting within. But no one had lurked in the shadows; no one had suspected anything; not a policeman had looked their way. They had lifted and carried and pulled and hauled, and at the end of the evening the yard had been full of bones. Edwin said that someone must have been adding other animals, because of the quantity. It hardly seemed possible that a human had just as many bones in him as a crocodile. By then it had been the number of them rather than the size that astonished and tired them. They were glad to drop the last drum of backbone and escape into the street, to walk stiffly home, too tired to speak, too full of activity done to think. Sleep had been washing the back of Ainsley's mind as he walked, as if his head were full of warm water.

That was only last night. It felt like no time he had ever really known. It was more like being the other side of some enormous impassable fence; not far in distance, perhaps, but a place there was no longer any access to.

He ate a very large breakfast, and felt like a giant again. He was even glad to see Alice, though his chief reason was so that he could find out where she would be all day.

"Pottering about," she said. "I hope you're going out."

"I think so," said Ainsley. The night before they had not been witful enough to arrange about today; but they certainly had to go and tidy up the bones. He waited about the house until ten o'clock, cleaning shoes and bringing in coal. Then he went out and walked towards Harold's house, which was the natural focus, though it was farther out of the town.

Harold was there with Bobby. They were waiting for one or two more. Harold brought out the key of the Grammar school gate.

"I must remember to clean the fingerprints off it before we leave it," he said.

"We want them to know who we are," said Bobby. "But not that sort of way, I know what you mean."

"We'll leave them a letter," said Harold. "Let's go on. I want to finish with that creature."

"If there's a thing you can see enough of, it's a thing that size," said Bobby. "What if they've cleaned it away by the time we get there?"

"I shan't care," said Harold. "I shan't care a bit."

They did not see the others. They had all the work to do themselves. They went in at the gate in the High Street, and round the corner, and saw what they had done. It was like a shipwreck, with great bones everywhere, as if the creature had blown up. Or it was as if a monstrous bird had dropped a dry eggshell and it had shattered into several hundred pieces. None of them had counted the bones, but the impression each one of them had was that there were hundreds.

"Tell you what," said Bobby. "We couldn't get our fingerprints off that lot."

"I expect you could," said Harold. "They dust it with a powder. They'd need a lot, though."

"I meant, we couldn't clean them off," said Bobby. "Not the exact opposite."

They were alone. Only the empty windows of the school looked out on them. No one could see directly in. Harold cleaned the key on his handkerchief and hung it in its place beside the double doors, so that he would not forget it later. Then they began moving all the bones yet again. The only one they did not shift was the skull, which was now sitting lost amongst the scattered members of the body.

"Back bones first," said Harold. "They're all numbered on the right side, so we can't get them wrong."

They assembled the bones of the back and tail,

arraying them behind the head, where they naturally belonged.

"Why have him straight?" said Bobby. "What about a graceful curve?"

"Crocodiles don't have graceful curves," said Harold. "And it wouldn't be necessary. This is the home of graceful curves, you grave case of idiocy."

After the bones they brought the ribs. "Where do they go?" said Harold. "Come here, Bobby, and let's have a look at how you're joined together. Is this your head?"

"Used to be," said Bobby. "And that's my ribs, according to general knowledge; and that's not a bone, that's my stomach, if you don't mind."

"I was worrying," said Harold. "This crocodile hasn't any hips, so you couldn't have had a graceful curve."

"I'm not going back on the Strand to look for a crocodile's hips," said Ainsley. "It'll have to manage without. Worms do."

"They're probably lying in the street somewhere, pretending to be a sculpture," said Bobby. "Modern art and all that."

They gained an idea of where to put the ribs, but it was not possible to make them stand up and support the backbone as they had done on the Strand. They laid them out rather in the manner of wings, arranging them evenly, so that at least they looked tidy. The heap of small bones, which had no particular and obvious home, they laid in a pile by themselves.

"There," said Bobby. "It doesn't look pretty, but it does its best. Let's go now."

"Haven't left them a note," said Harold. "What shall we put?"

" 'Bone jour'," said Ainsley. "That's French."

"Something sensible," said Harold. " 'Sorry about the fish', or something."

182

"Something to overpower Alice," said Ainsley. "I could think of something."

" 'For your exhibition'," said Bobby. "So long as that little one doesn't think I said it to her. It would be right for anyone."

Harold had a piece of paper in his pocket. He wrote on it with the brush and the red paint he had used to mark the bones. He thought such writing would be more suited to a serious occasion. FOR YOUR EXHIBITION. He put it among the teeth of the skull.

They went out into the High Street again, shutting the little gate after them. No one had noticed them.

The afternoon was tolerable. They knew they had finished, and they were still stiff and tired from the day before. Mother noticed that they had suddenly stopped going to the Strand, when Bobby and Harold came in and they watched the sports programme all the afternoon. Before tea the others went home. Ainsley stayed by the television set all the evening, and went to bed early with sleep catching his eyes and forcing them closed.

The next morning was Sunday. Ainsley had a sudden worry about church. They had had services one week in the Grammar school, and the next week in his, and that had been last week. Were they to return to the Grammar school this week? He worried about it until he had to ask. It was the sort of thing that would not occur to Harold, who had only been to church once at his own baptism. It was a worry that took him to dinner time, when he found that services were now to be in the church hall, until the future of the church was decided.

In the afternoon he found he was worse off, because Bobby was there, with Edwin. They both half-suspected Edwin of being about to say something, which was one worry; and they both had a more general worry about what was going to happen, and what would be said. There

183

was no way of getting out of it now. It was done. But worry will worry.

There was no rumour in church. No one came up and said, "Have you heard?" Both of them expected it any moment, and it never came.

"I'm going to school early," said Bobby. "I daren't go down the High Street when the girls are going in. I'd feel safer at school, if Miss Palmer wants to attack me. The old man would never allow it."

"He might have his own ideas," said Ainsley. "I hope this finds you as it grieves me. Bend over, my boy, and all that."

Ainsley was out before his usual time, ahead of Alice. Mother had looked at him at breakfast time and said he looked quite pale. She thought he must have caught a chill on the Strand, and almost wanted him to stay at home. Ainsley said he felt marvellous, but he had to convince himself. He would have liked to stay remote from the world in bed all day, and perhaps for a week or two, and let the world get over things without his help.

Bobby was even ahead of Ainsley. He turned when Ainsley called him, but he would not stop. Ainsley ran up to him, and they went on without thinking of Harold.

The High Street was the same as ever. There was nothing strange about it. The Grammar school gate was closed still. It looked as if it had not been opened yet. They passed by. A knot of girls approached, and went to the gate, and through it. There was no result. Nothing happened. There were no screams, there was no shout of rage. There was no Miss Palmer with a hockey stick or crocodile tusk.

"Something will happen during the day," said Bobby. "I feel it in my bones."

They waited for Harold in the form room. Other people came in and looked at their torn and patched blazers. Ainsley had managed to keep his from Mother's eye, but he had to wear it to school. He had brushed it and tacked a

184

gap together. Bobby had tidied his, but both were in equal disgrace.

Peter was in next. He was wearing a new blazer. "Couldn't get Saturday," he said. "Got a new blazer instead. I have to pay for it myself, and then buy it back out of my earnings."

Guy was apologetic too. He said he had slept what he called "all over the clock", and then stayed in bed till tea time. Derek had not known where to go, and he had not liked to wander into the Grammar school by himself; so he had gone home too, and watched his mother mend his blazer.

Harold came in, and checked his watch against the school clock. There were others there too, now, so they had to talk of other things.

The bell rang for assembly. The Headmaster came in, closed the window to keep out the east wind, wrapped his gown round himself, and began the school day. There was nothing unusual at all. He gave his top form a long look, but that was only their blazers. They could see him noting that he would say something later to them about that.

The morning was half gone when he came to the classroom and took all six of them out of it. He had a piece of paper in his hand, and several pieces of cloth. The reckoning had come. This was the tidal wave that might overcome them.

"I'm getting tired of this," he said. "Once this term I dealt with you for going into the Grammar school yard, and another time I dealt with you for interfering with the girls' pastimes in a rather offensive way. A dead fish, that time, I think. And now I gather that you have been in that yard again, and put a heap of bones there. I have here a handful of material of the same colour as your blazers. I saw your blazers this morning, so it wasn't difficult for me to guess that the people who left so much cloth behind would be the ones with rather less blazer to their backs this morning. *Are* you the ones?"

"Yes, sir," said Harold. There was only one way through this passage: straight through.

"I've got a new blazer, sir," said Peter. "I've got it on." He was under the impression, at the moment, that they were being told not to come to school in tatters.

"Yours must have been the worst of the lot," said the Headmaster.

"It was," said Peter.

"I'm bound to ask you whether there's an explanation," said the Headmaster. "But I don't think it would be fair for me to hear it. I try to think as well of you as I can. I try to make the most of your abilities for you. I try to teach you something before you leave school. I hope I have; but I don't think I've succeeded. Never have I met such obtuseness, such idiocy, such disregard of warnings. I am just wondering how to deal with you. I've been through my usual range of punishment. I've been lenient and I've been severe. I've given you warnings, I've made requests. And yet you go and do the very same thing for a second time. The very same thing. And not only one thing, but two. Twice you have disregarded the warnings your senses have given you. But I have said enough for now. I feel deeply ashamed that any pupil here could act as you have. Why should I, why should the school, be involved in your acts of hooliganism? I feel so strongly about it that we are all going down to the Grammar school now, and you are going to take those remains away and bury them. You need not think I shall enjoy parading through the streets and appearing at another school with a gang of idle, thought-less, senseless ruffians. Yes, ruffians. A disgrace to your parents, your school, your town, and yourselves."

There was nothing to be said. They marched off in pairs, with the Headmaster behind them. Ainsley longed to say that they were walking in crocodile, but it would have been frivolous, as well as dangerously provoking to the Head-master. Apart from that thought there was nothing much else in Ainsley's mind. He was more busy arranging an atti-tude, in case he needed one later on when he was expelled. He had never known anyone expelled yet, so he was not sure of the proper frame of mind.

They went up the High Street, and turned in at the gate of the school. They walked into the yard, and were halted. The Headmaster came up and thumped Harold in the back for standing slackly, and went ahead.

They saw him stop and stare. His feet stayed where they were, but the rest of him turned round and looked back.

"Stand at ease," he said, and walked on.

"Didn't know what to think," said Harold. "He was expecting a sheep, not that."

There was no time for more talk, because the Head-master came back. He was still barking at them, but only out of habit. The real anger had gone out of his voice.

"Attention," he said. "Right turn, forward march." He marched them into the yard, and halted them again. The skeleton was lying where they had put it, and did not seem disarranged in any way.

"And what do you think that is?" said the Headmaster, looking at Harold.

"A crocodile, sir," said Harold. "We dug it up on the Strand."

"You idiots," said the Headmaster. "About turn, quick march"; and he marched them out of the Grammar school, down the High Street, and back to their classroom. "Fall out," he said. "I'll see you later."

XX

"IF YOU ask me, it was a flop," said Harold, at dinner time. "No result, if you see what I mean."

"We haven't been expelled yet," said Bobby. "If that's what you mean."

"Oh, that," said Harold. "I don't call that a result. That's just what happens. I mean, I thought those girls would be out watching for us, or be at the windows, or something."

"I didn't look," said Bobby. "I was only just alive. By the time he'd gone off the boil we were facing the other way and trooping back here, white owl's feather and all."

"You're forgetting why we did it," said Harold. "You never ought to forget the reason for doing things."

After dinner there was still no call to the study. They waited about in the yard, wondering how soon it would come. It was no time to be rushing about, kicking a football, when any moment you might be called in for sentence.

"The juvenile equivalent of the death penalty," said Guy. "I know it doesn't mean anything, Harold. It just sounds right."

"Oh, it's all right," said Harold. "You must have misread it."

They were leaning on the outside railing, by the road, wondering which side of them they really wanted to be, when the first visitors came. They were two middle school girls from the Grammar school.

"Ho, look," said Bobby. "What are they doing down here?"

Harold began to lick his lips, ready to whistle. "Don't," said Ainsley. "The old man might be watching."

"Us or them?" said Harold. "I'd better not. We'll just gaze."

The two girls came past the railings, and instead of looking to the other side of the road in their usual tiresome and ignoring way, they looked straight in. One of them nudged the other and said something very quiet.

"Looking at you, Harold Harold Harold," said Bobby. "Stand up straight, man, shoulders back, smile."

"Fold your pleated tongue," said Harold. "They're probably looking at someone behind me. I've been caught before."

The girls stopped, and turned and went away. They were the first of a dozen, coming in twos and threes until they were outside the school, and then going away.

"This is results," said Harold. "Peter, give me your blazer. I look like a tramp in this one."

Peter grinned. The bell rang, and they went across the yard to go in to school. They were met on the steps by the Headmaster.

"Come here, you ruffians," he said. "I wish you looked a little more like humans, but I suppose you can't help it. Get inside and comb your hair and wash your faces and get the dust off your shoes, then come back here, at the double. DOUBLE, Knight, not a paralytic crawl."

Harold wrestled with an inky tap and ran cold water over his hands. It ran straight off again, so that he was able to shake them dry. "He's very cheerful," he said. "Probably gone to pick up a firing-squad."

It was better than a firing-squad. "Go round to the Grammar school," he said. "And behave yourselves. They seem to think you've done them a favour. And don't come back here this afternoon. I don't want to see you. And the best of luck." He turned round and went in, pacing off with his gown tight on his shoulders.

"How do you read him?" said Harold.

"Split personality," said Bobby. "Coming and going, and doesn't think he's doing either."

"Thank you, Guy," said Harold. "I think he's sending

190

us off to meet Miss Palmer. I say, girls, I vote we go back and get our hockey sticks."

They were not alone when they reached the Grammar school. There was a man in the yard already, taking a photograph of the bones, with the help of some seniors.

"Alice," said Ainsley. "And others like her. They used to bully me when I was a little boy."

"No, Miss Palmer," said Harold. "You boys smarten up. Peter, take that face off."

"My mum says I wasn't to take it off," said Peter. "Oh, my face. I aren't going to lend that either."

The man in the yard saw them and came towards them. "You the lads?" he said.

"I'm the new games mistress," said Harold. "These are my sisters."

"Blimey, kids," said the man. "Look, this heap of bones may be the year's big joke to you, but to me it's a heap of bones. Just tell me what I want to know, and I'll put in the funny bits."

"Why?" said Harold. "We're Beachcomber, not you."

The man laughed. "*Touché*," he said. "I don't mean to hustle you, but I want to put these plates on the train and write up what I can, and then go to a Council meeting and an old lady of a hundred, so I'm a bit pushed."

"This is our old lady of a million," said Bobby.

"I can't keep up with six of you," said the man. "I just represent a news service, so I'll ask you a few questions. Where did you get this whatever it is?"

"Out on the Strand," said Harold.

"Strand," said the man. "I know it. Go on."

"It was buried in a sand-dune."

"Dune," said the man. "Go on. What is it?"

Gradually he drew the story out of them, picking it as clean as the skeleton itself. He took half an hour over it, and then posed them by the bones and photographed them. He made Ainsley and Alice, when he knew they were brother and sister, hold up one of the ribs, whilst he arranged an interesting angle.

"Right," he said, in the end. "I'll do my best for you."

"That'll be a change," said Harold. "Actually, we aren't doing so badly now."

"Good," said the man, pulling a plate out of his camera. Then he went, after a nod all round.

Miss Palmer came out then, and stood as a barrier between girls and boys. "You'll have been here long enough," she said. "Long enough for today, shall we say?"

"We were sent round here," said Bobby.

"Not by me," said Miss Palmer. "If they don't want you at your school, we still don't want you at ours."

Miss Palmer gathered her flock of seniors and took them in. The boys began to go away, after they had fussily put straight some bones they thought were slightly out of place. At the gate they met another man.

"Wrong place," he said. "Go back." He was not talking to the boys, but to someone following him, carrying a box on a tripod. "Looking for the girls' Grammar school," he said.

"This is it," said Harold. "They've all gone in now."

He would have gone past and out, but the man stopped him. "Are you one of those boys?" he said. "Come back if you are. We want to know something about you. Television news, Northern Lights, the programme that might bring you to yourself any night of the year."

"I know you," said Harold. "You're not the same, real."

"I am," said the man. "The only man who shaves himself at a monitor. Where's this giant crocodile? Bring that camera, George, take these kids. Walk down there. Is that it? Couldn't you find a bigger one? Walk down to it. Don't look round. Stop. Go when I say so. Go." They heard him talking into a microphone. Then the camera clicked to a stop, and he came across to the bones to join them.

"I've got a bone to pick with you," he said. "You must

192

have heard that. No? I'll put it in. Say it just before they think of it themselves, it's funny. Say it just after, it's funny. Say it at the same time, you're dull. Our advantage, we choose what we show you. Get down to business. Where are the girls? Never mind, can't bear schoolgirls. Nor can George. Can't bear schoolgirls, can you, George?"

"Never went to school," said George. "Rather bear chorus girls."

"Joke," said the other man. "You know my name, Andy Chalk. Now you tell me your names, you, you, you, you, you, you."

As fast as they said them he wrote them down. He looked round at George. "Got it?" he said. "Good. Get some more about you in a bit. Now what about your skeleton? Came out of a big cupboard, did that. Begin at the beginning."

Harold was beginning to catch up with this man. "It was an egg first," he said.

"Marmalade me," said Andy Chalk. "I know. Is this a yolk? I know you didn't grow it from a chick, lad. How did you come by it?"

Once more the story had to be told. This time it came a little differently, with the camera flitting from face to face, and Andy Chalk putting in his jokes just before or just after everyone else had thought of them. But he never stopped writing.

"Right," he said. "Just carry one of those bones about. That skull, alas poor Yorick. There's plenty of you."

There was more film taken as they tried to move the skull, without any success, of course.

"Now," said Andy Chalk. "That's what you did. One of you go and fetch some of the girls. Don't pick and choose, any sort will do. The scruffier they are the more they're like our little Emily."

"We can't go in there," said Bobby. "They've just sent us out of here."

"Then why did you bring this in?" said Andy Chalk.

"So the girls would notice us," said Harold. "But they haven't yet."

"Nice," said George.

A bell rang in the school, and the doors opened. The girls were coming out. "Get behind me, you boys," said Andy Chalk. "Cover that flood, George. Now drop it a bit and get some heads in the top of the picture. I'll clear a way through to the bones."

He began to organize the crowd of girls, making a way through them so that there was a vista of bones beyond the navy blue of school tunic. He sent the boys down to lift up a rib to frame the top of the picture. Then he caught a junior and asked her what she thought the bones were. She said it was a fossil, and when he asked her she said she thought she would play on it.

"Fine," said George.

"You boys stay here, unless you've anything against it," said Andy Chalk. "I'm going in search of the Headmistress. I shan't want you again."

They sat on the ribs, and waited for beautiful friendships to form automatically. They were looked at a good deal, and that was all. No one spoke to them, and they did not know what to say to the girls. Still it was pleasant to be here, Ainsley thought. It was like an ideal kind of zoo.

The bell rang again, and they were once more alone. They were getting cold, standing or sitting. Andy Chalk and George came out of the school, gave them a wave, and went out of the gate.

At home, when Alice arrived, there was a silence between her and Ainsley.

"Do you know what he's done, Mother?" said Alice.

"No," said Mother. "Should he have?"

"I don't know," said Alice. "It's rather an odd thing. He found a fossil, and they put it in our yard."

194

"You didn't show it me, Ainsley," said Mother. "What is it of?"

"He says it's a crocodile," said Alice. "And it's so big that they must have made it themselves. Crocodiles aren't that big, I'm sure."

"That one is," said Ainsley. "It has jaws eleven feet long, and twenty-six pairs of teeth, with five missing. We counted them. It hasn't got any back legs, that's all. Who would make a thing like that?"

"That's a funny question from a church-going boy," said Mother. "Tell me about it."

So at home it settled with hardly a ripple. Alice thought it was the sort of thing that Ainsley did without succeeding in necessarily being naughty. Mother had not grasped the size of the thing, and Dad said he would come and see it, but wanted his tea now. They both seemed to see crocodiles as low, flat creatures, more like logs, and not really of a bony nature at all.

"We'll see whether it's a new one tomorrow," said Alice. "The man's coming to see it. The same one that saw mine and thought it was a new kind, Dr Wells. I wonder if he'll know tomorrow."

The next morning Mother was upstairs shaking Ainsley's shoulder before Alice's alarm went. She had the morning paper in her hand, and she was pointing to a picture on the front page. Ainsley looked at the picture. It was no one he knew, and he said so.

"It's you," said Mother. "You, on the front page. 'Boys find giant lizard on Yorkshire beach. Yesterday I heard a remarkable story from the lips of six remarkable boys.'"

"Shut up, Mother," said Ainsley. "Is that me?"

"I ought to know you," said Mother. "But where's this crocodile?"

"We're holding it up," said Ainsley. "Look, there's Harold and Bobby. I didn't see them at first."

195

"I still can't see the crocodile," said Mother. "I'm like Captain Hook."

That was the moment for Alice's alarm to ring, which made her more like Captain Hook than ever. Ainsley traced the big rib bone with his finger. "Him," he said. "That's a rib."

"One rib," said Mother. "That big? I'm glad it's dead."

Alice read the paper with a sort of scorn. "There's nothing about me," she said, "I'm glad to say."

"I'm sure you are, dear," said Mother.

The Headmaster was in his mood today that forced him to keep his hands on his hips and his elbows out. He would walk about like that and you had to keep out of his way. Some days he felt a little larger than life, and this was one of them. He came into assembly obviously feeling twice as large as usual. Harold had carefully closed the open window by the platform, to keep the good mood going. The Headmaster strode cheerfully across to it and flung it open. "Can't have all this frowst in here," he said, and went all round the wall turning off the radiators. Harold put up his blazer collar against the cold wind; but put it down again when he found that the wind was not cold. It was warm. The Headmaster grinned cheerfully and told everyone the wrong hymn, and had a happy little argument about it with the master at the piano.

After assembly he stopped the top form, and held back the usual six. "Well," he said, "they're going to christen your crocodile today. You'd better go round and stand godfather to it."

"Sir," said Harold, because the Headmaster's mood had changed so with the climate, "he might be an ancestor. We can't be godfather to an ancestor."

"You do what I tell you," said the Headmaster. "And heaven preserve me from television."

He added that he did not want to see them until dinner

196

time, and then he would tell them what he thought of them. But he had certainly lost the edge of his temper.

They understood better when they were outdoors again. Harold had felt the wind warm at the window. Going to school had been as cold as ever, but the wind had changed in half an hour, and came now out of the west, warm and full of wetness, so that pavements and windows and cars were bloomed over with dew, settling at the wrong end of the day.

They met Alice in the High Street. She was expecting them. She had come out, she said, to meet Dr Wells, who had looked at her crocodile, and was about to look at theirs. He was supposed to have come on the train, but had not arrived yet.

"We know what he looks like," said Ainsley. "We met him before you."

"He'll have gone out on the Strand again," said Bobby. "That's what made him late last time. We'll fetch him for you."

"You're supposed to be here when he comes," said Alice. "Didn't they tell you?"

"Yes," said Bobby. "But since they're going to expel us, it doesn't matter whether we obey or not."

They found Dr Wells by the station, walking back from the Strand, and led him back to the Grammar school. All the way he talked about the change in the weather, saying he had woken up very cross at having his routine disturbed; but whilst he walked on the Strand the wind had moved and he had felt like a new man, almost, he said, as if he was about to see a vision.

Alice greeted him properly, and took him into the school through the front door, which was in the High Street, not in the yard. The boys had to go into the yard.

The bones, which had been cold, were dewed with the same sweet dew. They were too wet to sit on; but it was not too cold to stand about.

After a time Alice led Dr Wells out of the yard door. With them came the other members of the Natural History group. Dr Wells was trying to walk right across the yard, but Alice led him to the bones.

Dr Wells looked at them, touched the skull, bent over to look at the teeth more carefully, paced the length of the skeleton, and then walked back to the watching group, smiling. He opened his mouth to speak, but was overcome with laughter. It was an infectious laugh, and they caught it from him, and they stood in a semi-circle with tears on their faces. Dr Wells tried to speak again, waving his hand towards the skull. He was choked by laughter again.

"Poor sense of humour," he said at last. "Sorry you've had all that trouble for nothing. Can't help laughing. That's not a crocodile . . ." He was bellowing with laughter now and tears were not running down his face but splashing straight from his eyes on to the ground. "Not a 'dile. It's a whale, a sperm whale, a cachalot, *Physeter catodon*; and it's not even a fossil. It's quite new, not a hundred years old." He wiped his eyes and straightened his face. "Forgive me," he said. "I thought I might see visions, and I did. What a lot of trouble you must have had, digging that thing up, and all to no purpose. How long did it take?"

"We saw it the last time you were here," said Harold. "We came to the station to ask you about it, but the train had gone."

"What a pity," said Dr Wells. "I could have told you in a moment, and saved you such a lot of trouble. I say, please forgive me for laughing. It just struck me as funny. I'm not supposed to have a very good sense of humour."

"It's all right," said Harold. "We'd have brought it just the same if we'd thought it was a whale. But whales don't have faces like that, do they?"

"Ah," said Dr Wells. "That's only the bone. All the

square front of *Physeter catodon* is blubber. Its skeleton is very different from its outer shape."

Then he set to and explained whales, which he seemed to know as much about as he did fossils.

XXI

THEY were all seeing Dr Wells to the midday train. They had taken him out on the Strand, with Alice and the other girls, and walked back along the railway, across the level crossing, and down to the station, where the train was waiting, its steam rising in the moist air of newly begun spring.

"It's been a very pleasant morning," said Dr Wells, leaning from his carriage window. "I'm sorry it wasn't a fossil. That would have been much more interesting. But your little one, the real crocodile, is certainly new to me. I haven't quite fitted it in yet, but when I do I'll have a christening party, and a real one at that."

"Have you finished?" said Mr Knight, Peter's father, who was waiting to let the train go. He did not want to inconvenience his only passenger.

"Yes, it's time I went," said Dr Wells. "Good-bye, and let me know if you find anything else."

"I will," said Alice. "Let me know about *Steneosaurus*."

"A bargain," said Dr Wells.

The train said "Baff, bafbafbafbafbafbaf, baff", and began to move away. Dr Wells put his window half up, and went out of sight.

"Good, he's not hanging out," said Bobby. "It's very embarrassing when people wave back all the way to the next station. I always feel silly waving back, and mean if I don't."

"Let's wave at nothing," said Harold, "and appear to be grave cases of madness."

"Do what you like," said Alice. "We're going back to school. Do you want to walk down with us? As far as the gate?"

"No," said Ainsley.

"Yes," said Harold. "Don't we?"

They were gradually finding things to talk about to the girls. They had begun the morning in silence, except that Dr Wells was saying a good deal about geology and palaeontology. They had listened; but in between they had only looked at the girls they were walking along with. They had not known what to say. As time went on they forgot that strangers were there, and when they reached the dune the whale had come from and had dug again for any remaining bones with their bare hands they had found they were talking easily, about ordinary things like the names of cats and television and the weather, or kinds of ink, and mothers' maiden names and whether they liked Alice, or what records were the best of the latest top ten, and favourite subjects and games.

The only thing each side was not sure of were the names of the ones on the other. When they came down into the High Street again even that was made clearer, because the girls had the sudden idea of buying a copy each of the paper with Ainsley's picture in, and getting him to sign the margin with a hook-billed pen belonging to one of them. It made bad blots on the thirsty paper. Harold and Bobby were in the background of the picture, each recognizing the other but not himself. They signed too, and took the opportunity, which Ainsley had neglected, of taking the girls' names and addresses. Alice had not bought a newspaper. She threatened to box Bobby's ears if he wrote down her name and address.

"Ah," said Harold, when they were alone again. "Let's go and find another whale."

The Headmaster came across to their table at dinner. "And another thing," he said. "What about last Friday?"

They all stopped eating. They had forgotten about Friday.

"Ill, sir?" said Harold. "No?"

"No," said the Headmaster. "Stop being a fool, Tewgon.

I must tell you that I am going to see the Governors this afternoon, and I'm bound to report to them about this whole affair. So don't be too blasé and confident. We can't have the whole school skylarking and doing what they like. It wouldn't be sense."

Harold finished his pudding in silence. "He won't do it," he said. "He only says it to worry us. The trouble is, it does."

They were almost sure that the Headmaster was pleased with them, in a way. But almost sure is not certain. There was still something of the condemned cell about school.

On the way home Ainsley remembered another thing, and put it from him again. He would bear that when it came. It might not come. Meanwhile he had to bear Alice, who was chuckling about the crocodile that wasn't even a fossil.

"I'm not laughing at you," said Alice. "I just think it was funny. I thought it must be a crocodile too. I thought whales had aertex mouths and strained shrimps through. I didn't know they had teeth. I was jealous. I still am."

"The weather's improved you," said Ainsley. "Has it improved me?"

"I can bear you," said Alice. "The east wind always makes me cross. You ought to know by now. Which do you want on, ITV or BBC?"

"Don't mind," said Ainsley. "Whichever you like. ITV, please. I want to watch Northern Lights."

"I always like that too," said Mother.

"I'd like it tonight too," said Alice. Generally she disdained ITV and would only watch BBC, because it was the fashion in the top form at school. Today she was being kind to everyone.

Dad had put his feet by the fire, and was going to watch ITV with them when there was a knock at the door. It was Mr Merriott. He came in and sat down. Alice turned the television low. Ainsley wondered whether to go out straight away, or whether to stay and be reminded of how they had dug up Mr Merriott's road in the face of his opposition.

"Turn that off, Alice," said Dad; but just at that moment the spongy music of Northern Lights died down, and Andy Chalk appeared on the screen.

". . . Bringing you tonight the affair of the old-age pensioner and her dog; the beginnings of a new industrial estate on Teesside; a genuine monster from the coast; and . . ."

"Turn it up," said Ainsley. "Listen, listen, listen."

Andy Chalk started with the monster. Mr Merriott sat and watched with them, without having said a word so far. There was a shot of six of them walking across the Grammar school yard, with Andy Chalk talking, and introducing the subject. They saw Ainsley and Harold heaving up a bone, and all of them pulling at the skull. Then there was a full-size picture of Harold saying that he had put the bones where he did so that they could get to know the girls, followed by more wit from Andy Chalk, and a picture of the yard filling with girls. Then there was some stately speech from the Headmistress, and a few breezy words from the Headmaster of Ainsley's school. The last question was: "What punishment do you propose to give them?"

"Nothing," said the Headmaster. "I think they're a credit to the school but I shan't tell them so just yet, or they might get swelled heads."

"No question of expulsion?" said Andy Chalk.

"None at all," said the Headmaster, and swung the sleeve of his gown over his shoulder.

"Well I never," said Ainsley.

"And a last word from a scientist," said Andy Chalk. "Dr Wells, you have seen this creature. Is it a crocodile?"

"No, indeed," said Dr Wells. "I saw it this morning. I laughed like a drain. It is the skeleton of a sperm whale, and a very good one too . . ."

"So much for monsters," said Andy Chalk. "And now to a more serious question: Should old age pensioners keep a dog on National Assistance?"

Alice turned the voice off, and watched very old people being ordered about by their dogs. Mr Merriott stood up again.

"I had just come to see you about something," he said. "But I've thought about it since I came in, and now I don't think it matters a bit." He looked straight at Ainsley. Ainsley looked back and dropped his eyes. Mr Merriott had won. But at least he had won privately. Having won he went, with apologies for troubling them.

"Very odd," said Dad. "He's very shy, of course."

"It wasn't that," said Ainsley. "I will now tell you everything about everything, and all the wrong things we did."

"It's all right," said Alice. "I shan't listen. I'm going to do my homework."

205

Ainsley took a deep breath. "You can listen if you want," he said. "It's your kettle of fish too."

Alice opened her mouth to correct him on the point that whales are not fish, but shut it before she said so. "Spout," she said. "That's the right word."